Dangerous To Know

Other titles by Katy Moran:

katy moran

Dangerous to know

WALKER
BOOKS

First published in Great Britain 2011 by Walker Books Ltd
87 Vauxhall Walk, London SE11 5HJ

2 4 6 8 10 9 7 5 3 1

Text © 2011 Katy Moran

This book has been typeset in Fairfield

Printed and bound in Great Britain by Clays Ltd, St Ives plc

British Library Cataloguing in Publication Data:
a catalogue record for this book is
available from the British Library

ISBN 978-1-4063-1729-9

www.walker.co.uk

www.katymoran.co.uk

This book is dedicated to those
Divine and Delicious girls

Bubsie, Jules, Rosie and Annabel

SOMETIME IN THE 1990s

ONE

So, there was this little festival thing the second weekend in June. It was going to be easy. Sammy's parents were doing the vegetarian café plus the watermill demonstrations (his mum was also selling Mooncups, and I don't know what they are but I've got this bad feeling they're something rough). Anyway, Sammy wangled five wristbands off them. Enough for everyone: me, Jono, Sammy – and Bethany. Sammy sold the fifth to some guy in the lower sixth. Our plan was foolproof, absolutely watertight: Mum and Louis were in France till the Wednesday after (some wedding I'd managed to get out of, to Louis' blatant relief); Jono told his mum he was staying at mine; Bethany's parents were under the mistaken apprehension that she was on an Art field trip to the coast with her school. Sammy's mum and dad had got us the wristbands, so they were no bother. Bethany's cover was by far the most audacious.

I had known her for just under a month. The second time we met, in the playground outside the bowls club, I said, "There's this festival in a couple of weeks. My mate can get free tickets. Come if you like."

I had expected her to look at me like I was some kind of freak – after all, she barely knew met. But Bethany smiled and said, "All right."

She had guts. She was fearless. Most of the time. We stood there looking at each other for what seemed like ages. I felt as if I'd known her before.

It was meant to be simple. What actually happened was this. First of all we couldn't get a lift with Sammy's parents because they'd gone down the night before to set up and wouldn't let him take the Friday off school. So it was the train. We stopped to buy fags on the way to the station and missed the first one, managed to catch the second, but it was a stopper and took two godforsaken hours. Then no one had any money (not to spend on train tickets, anyway – total rip off), so we had to hide in the bogs for the whole time: Jono and Sammy, me and Bethany. We couldn't smoke and we couldn't make any noise. The last thing you want is for the ticket collector to figure out you're in there. They're not idiots. They know what people do.

So I was trapped in an enclosed space with a beautiful girl, it was obvious what we should have been doing. Well, we didn't. It stank. I'm not going to romance a girl in a train toilet that reeks of piss. So we played scissors, paper, stone for ages (Bethany won most times, but women are more intuitive, aren't they?), and when we were sure the ticket inspector wasn't around, we talked. Quite a lot about her dad.

Bethany could talk about anything, and I never got bored listening to her. She didn't go on about TV and celebrities like most of the girls at my school. Clearly, though, the first thing I liked about her was the way she looked: long, shiny black hair, dark eyes, weird clothes she'd mashed together on a second-hand sewing machine, fake flowers pinned in her hair that she'd stitched by hand out of bits of silk from old dresses and stuff. Bethany was different. I can still remember, too, what she was wearing that evening we caught the train with Sammy and Jono: black wellingtons (we were going to a festival), old grey school tights, a dress made of flowy pink material that felt cool like water and a bright green coat done up with a brooch in the shape of spider. She was also wearing a woolly hat, even though it was June.

"This is going to sound bad," Bethany was saying leaning against the sink, "but when Dad first got ill, I was actually angry with him." She stared down at her hands: she wore a ring with a jewel thing made up of tiny multi-coloured beads and her fingernails were painted blue. "It made Mum so overprotective. I know that's really selfish of me but it's true. She wouldn't even let me cycle to school any more: I had to get a lift in her enormous bloody car."

I shrugged. "That's not selfish. You're just being honest." Bethany loved her bike; I didn't know anyone else who rode one except my massively sad stepdad, Louis.

One of the first times I saw Bethany she was riding across the park, black hair everywhere, and I had to stop and watch her go by. Then a couple of hours later there was Bethany at Amanda Blake's birthday party with bike oil all over her skirt. She was standing in the sitting room with Mands' cousin from the girls' school, smoking a roll-up and drinking a bottle of red wine. Everyone else was on the White Lightning. I couldn't stop staring at her. Mands' cousin Amelia is a bit of a geek and nothing to look at – weird fluffy hair, shiny face, glasses, played about fourteen different instruments – but Bethany was something else. Really.

"Jack, what are you doing, you loser?" Jono hissed at me. "She's going to think you're some kind of psycho."

"What the fuck are you talking about?" I asked him. He should have known better.

Jono passed me a fag and said, "Look, sorry, mate, but you know what I mean. Anyway, look at her friend for Christ's sake. She's obviously a loser."

Jono was wrong anyway, because Bethany and I ended up doing the washing-up together. Well, she went off to do it and I followed her. If you see a chance, take it. All the other girls were wearing jeans, grandad shirts – Bethany's oil-streaked skirt was white with a silver pattern. She had a Radiohead T-shirt over a tight long-sleeved top with black and white stripes. Nothing matched. She stood out from the others like a Christmas decoration catching the light. We stood at the sink in Mands' kitchen. I'd put in too much washing up liquid; my arms were invisible up to the elbow, lost in a mound of bubbles.

"You idiot." Bethany laughed. Her glittery eye make-up had spread across her face. "Boys are all the same. You only need a tiny bit. I bet you never wash up at home."

"What, do you think I'm doing it just to impress you?"

"Maybe."

I scooped out a handful of soapsuds and blew them into her face. Bethany laughed again. The bubbles were white against her black hair, rainbow-sheened, and I had to catch my breath; I suddenly felt as if the air had been knocked clean out of my lungs.

I wanted to take hold of her; I wanted her to reach for me.

But what if she turned away? I didn't have the courage, not yet.

I took a long, steadying breath. "Did you see Radiohead on tour last year, then?" I asked her, feeling like a massive idiot.

Bethany just smiled, glancing down at her top. "Yep, been there – got the T-shirt. It was amazing, though."

"There's so much crap music around you've got to take your chance if something good comes up."

We talked for a while about the rubbish commercial stuff that gets played everywhere, and Bethany said, "I wish I'd been around in the sixties. Not just the music but everything else – there was so much going on. Now there's just – nothing."

I laughed. "Especially here. So why did you move to this shitheap of a town, anyway?" I handed her a pint glass to dry, glancing at the clock on the oven. We'd been talking for over an hour, and I silently thanked God we'd all made such a mess. I've never been more glad to take time over the washing-up.

Bethany paused, polishing the glass with her tea towel. "My dad's job." She turned away; I just caught sight of her expression – she looked so afraid. She lifted her head, smiling again, but there was something brittle about it, as if she was wearing a glass mask over her true face.

"And you're right, this place is rubbish," Bethany said, brightly. "But what can a girl do, eh?"

"Wait," I said. "Did I say something wrong?"

"Are we washing up, or what?" Bethany held out her tea towel.

"No, hold on. You looked really weirded out. Are you OK?" I shrugged. "You don't have to tell me or anything. I just thought, well, you know…" I trailed off. *God, she's going to think I'm a real loser now*, I thought. Why hadn't I kept my mouth shut?

Bethany reached into the sink, took out the last glass. We were nearly finished. "My dad got a new job but he's not working at the moment. He's off. Having treatment. He's got cancer. Just after we moved. The chemo makes him really sick."

"Oh," I said. "That's shitty luck. I'm really sorry." The smell of weed drifted in beneath the kitchen door. But by the sound of it, most people had left.

Bethany shrugged, half laughing. "Yep. You could definitely say it was shitty luck. I can't believe I just told you that. You're the first person here. I talk to my friends back home all the time, but it's not the same. And the girls at school – you know. It's hard. It's not like I want people to feel sorry for me."

"Where did you live before?" I wanted to give her an escape route: I hate it when people try and force me to talk about personal things if I don't want to.

"North London," Bethany told me. "It was cool. We used to go to Camden Market, Portobello Road. There's loads of stuff to do."

I raised my eyebrows. "Unlike this hellhole."

"Yes, well. It's not that bad, I suppose. It's pretty. How long have you lived here?"

I shrugged. "For ever. But I'm leaving the minute I get the chance."

"Are you?" Bethany asked, and for a moment we both just stood facing one another.

"You've still got bubbles in your hair," I said. We were closer now. I don't even know how that happened. Her eyes were brown, the lashes dark and heavy.

"Well," said Bethany, "and whose silly fault is that?"

Looking at her was like staring straight at the sun: I couldn't take it. I glanced away a second, trying to get a grip, but I could smell her skin – something chocolatey, lemony, hot.

And that was it. I couldn't stop myself; I had to hold her. I didn't care if her mate was a geek or she was weird. *If she knocks me back, I'll die*, I thought, but Bethany didn't.

It was like diving into a deep warm pool from miles high, going in for that kiss, not knowing if she was going to turn away, and then when she didn't I felt like I was flying. The location wasn't exactly romantic or exotic but I wasn't complaining. Her mouth tasted of Jelly Tots and cigarette smoke.

I was hungry for more.

The train rattled along, and Bethany played with the soap dispenser, squirting thick pink goo into the plastic fag-burned basin. Then she turned to me. "Do you really think I'm not being selfish coming with you guys this weekend? I do. I should be more worried about Dad, not thinking about myself the whole time."

I know how it feels to be afraid that someone you love is going to die.

Bethany's eyes burned into me and, for a moment, I thought she might ask me about Owen and Herod. Everyone in our town knows about them, what they did and what came after. This place is just a hole in the ground where nothing happens, so people still talk about my brothers and use them as bogeymen to frighten their kids, even five years later. *Watch out, you don't want to end up like that MacNamara boy*. Then quite often they'll mutter something like, *You'd think their father would have done* something, *with all that money*. My family has become a cautionary tale. When both Herod and Owen were gone, Mum even went into school to speak at an assembly about the Dangers of Drugs. That was before I started, thank Christ. I'm not cool enough to survive an onslaught like that. As if having a crazy brother wasn't enough to deal with.

"Look," I said, "you're only human. Don't feel guilty. It isn't your fault and you've got to have some fun. Maybe your mum feels like she's got to control something, since she can't do anything to help your dad."

I didn't know then how much of a bitch Bethany's mother was, or I wouldn't have defended her with my pop psychology. Turned out she was worse than my dad, and he's an evil old hippy with more money than God.

For a moment, Bethany just stared at me. I couldn't read the expression on her face at first. Then I realized she looked grateful, somehow, as if I'd just handed her my last bottle of water in the middle of the desert. "Jack—" she started to say, but the train stopped with a jolt. We both slammed into the toilet door, clutching at each other and laughing.

I peered out of the window at the sign on the platform. "This is it. Come on."

TWO

Casual as you like, we stopped to let an old lady get off the train first (I even lifted her tartan shopping trolley down onto the platform), and there we were, along with a few pikey-looking types clearly also on their way to the festival. We're on a branch line, not the London one, otherwise it probably would've been loads more crowded. I saw Jono and Sammy hanging around by the Coke machine near the waiting room. Jono was lighting a fag; Sammy was rolling one. Bloody idiots: they should have got out of the station quicker, before anyone asked to see a ticket.

"All right?" said Sammy. "No hassle from the guard?"

Bethany shook her head. "We just kept quiet."

Sammy smiled and went a bit red. Jono said nothing. I think he had decided to pretend that Bethany wasn't there.

When I'd told them she was coming with us, Jono was like, "That freaky-looking posh bird from Mands' crappy party? You asked her? Jack, she'll whinge and moan the whole time. She'll probably want to bring her servants with her or something. You're such a dick."

Sammy had laughed. You're just jealous. She's fit. He's scored, all right? Get over it."

We bundled out of the station and went into Spar to get some cider. Bethany paid for it: girls always seem to get away with that stuff more easily (we gave her the money, though). To be honest, before we left town I hadn't thought about how we were going to get to the actual festival. When we got off the train, I reckoned maybe we'd follow some crusties from the station, but by the time we came out of the shop there was nobody around. It was a pretty small village: just the shop, an old man's pub and some thatched cottages strung out along one road.

Sammy passed the cider to Bethany but she shook her head, digging around in her backpack instead.

"Come on," Jono said, "we should get going. What time did your mum say we had to be at the gate for?"

"Ten at the latest." Sammy was looking a bit worried: it was quarter to nine already. "They don't let anyone in after that and Mum said it's about five miles from here."

"Ah, we've got ages," Jono said. I don't think he'd ever actually walked one mile before, let alone five.

I had, but I wasn't worried. There was no way we were

going to get on site by ten, but we were young and fit (well, kind of – if you didn't count the lovely smoker's cough). Anyway, we could climb a fence if we had to.

"Just let me have a look at this, or we won't find it at all." Bethany pulled an Ordnance Survey map out of her rucksack, unfolding it as Jono hooted with laughter. Across the street, a woman opened the front door of her cottage, put out a couple of milk bottles and glared at us. We were drawing too much attention to ourselves already.

Bethany ignored Jono, turning to Sammy. "Where did your mum say we should meet her?"

I was pretty impressed by the map. I smiled at her and started rolling a joint with the lovely sticky I'd got off Buggy the Dealer. This is actually a bit embarrassing, and no one knows, but last term I paid a Goth guy in the upper sixth a fiver to teach me how to skin up. Then I showed Jono and Sammy. Sammy could've asked his dad or his sister but didn't want to. A man's got to have some independence.

Sammy frowned, leaning over the map. "There it is on the main road, look. The staff gate is the first one you come to. We've got blue wristbands so it should be fine. But we should have been there, like, fifteen minutes ago. Mum told me to take a taxi from the station, gave me the number of one and everything."

"Well, where's the number? Let's call it." Jono stamped out his fag butt on the pavement and took a drag of cider, passing me the bottle.

Sammy grinned. "Lost it. Anyway, there's no phone box, is there?"

"Waste of money," I said. "Let's walk."

So we did.

By about eleven we'd found the festival site, thanks to Bethany and her Bronze Duke of Edinburgh Award, and we were utterly knackered. It was hilly round there. Even Sammy was moaning about his feet, and mine were killing me, too. Luckily, we were also quite drunk and slightly stoned, so no one was cold. The cider was bloody heavy: it made more sense to drink it, but we'd had to stop what seemed like a hundred times; five minutes after one of us had gone for a piss, someone else would need one and this was pretty funny, but maybe you had to be there. We'd been able to hear the music for about half an hour before we got within striking distance: a dull, low beat getting louder.

"There's the blue gate," Bethany said. We hung back near the hedge, not wanting to be spotted by the guys in fluorescent yellow coats.

"I could go and tell them we're on the staff list," Sammy said, sounding hopeful. "They might let us in even though the gate's shut. Mum's bound to have remembered to put us on. She got in a right stress about it."

But just then a knackered old Ford Transit pulled up right by the gate, blinding us with its headlights on full beam. "Hi, mate," I heard the driver say in this really posh voice. "We're staff. Shantih Café. I've got a van full of chocolate brownies that need to get into the fridge within the hour."

"Sorry, mate, I can't let you in here. Cut-off was ten p.m."

"It's not even eleven yet. We got stuck in traffic outside Bristol. Listen, can't you get hold of Damian? Damian Rhys-Edwards? He's site manager."

"Gate opens again at eight-thirty tomorrow, mate."

"I'm sorry, but can you just radio Damian? Or Rebecca? We really need to get in tonight. I can't lose this stock. I've got a thousand chocolate brownies back there."

"Sorry, mate."

"Shit," whispered Jono, "They're being really strict. What are we going to do?" His voice sounded kind of ragged and strung out. I hoped he wasn't going to lose the plot.

"It's cool," I said, very quietly. "Don't worry." About a hundred yards past the gate, I could see white give-way markings painted on the road and a shadowy gap in the hedge: a lane running parallel to the site.

I beckoned to the others and walked right past the gate while the chocolate brownie guy was still arguing with security. I didn't look behind me, but I sensed Bethany, Jono and Sammy following. We scarpered down the lane, filled with sudden terror that the fluorescent blokes might have spotted us after all and become suspicious.

It was time to stage a break-in.

THREE

All this began with a sofa Mum got from the small ads in the back of the paper. She needed a hand to lift it and Louis had a faculty meeting that night, so I met her at the hospital after school. She was running late, as usual. I sprawled in a canteen chair with a cup of black coffee – the least toxic thing I could find on the menu – trying not to breathe the scent of burnt cheese and disinfectant. It's no smoking in there so I was gasping for a fag, but not desperate enough to stand out in the rain like the old dudes leaning on Zimmer frames by the fire escape, cheerfully gasping their last.

I was the only customer except a couple of women. One was that sour-faced heifer Nadine who works on the reception desk. Every time I went in, she looked at me like I was going to nick her handbag. The other I'd never seen before.

She was a proper Kronenbourg – a real 1664. You know, sixteen and hot as hell from the back, ancient from the front. Never fails to make me feel a bit sick. Nadine talked and talked, not noticing or not caring that 1664 was clearly thinking about something else, tearing a leaflet into long, thin strips. I could people-watch for hours.

I looked up at the sound of a door opening on tired hinges and saw Mum dashing out of her office at the far end of the corridor. She ran into the canteen, belted over to the water cooler and filled a plastic cup, smiling at me over her shoulder, mouthing, *Sorry*, and holding up one hand, fingers spread. *I'll be five minutes.*

I didn't even have time to answer before Mum sped off back to her office, silver bracelets clinking as she half ran, half walked, splashing the water as she went. Sighing, I reached in my bag for my pad and started sketching the old horror in charge of the canteen till. She looked like a rotting potato in a hairnet so her face was pretty interesting to draw – full of weird lines and shadows – and I was getting really into it.

That was why it took me a while to realize that 1664 and Nadine were talking about me. Well, not me exactly, but my family. Nadine had her back to me; she didn't know I was there. They both stared down the corridor after Mum, even though she'd shut the office door again. 1664 had left the leaflet half-shredded on the table, listening now.

"It just goes to show money can't buy you everything,"

Nadine said. "The ex-husband's got it coming out of his ears, apparently, but what could he do?"

1664 turned slightly, eyes skimming over me as she stared after my mother, lips slightly pursed. Mum's got all this curly hair and a massive friendly smile (when she's not in one of her moods) and wears a lot of glittery Indian scarves. Even in her work clothes she doesn't look smart. *I'm naturally scruffy*, she'll always say. *That's my problem*. She'd ironed her blue shirt that morning, but it was wrinkled now. Her bright green leather shoes, always scuffed, were made by Guatemalan women in a co-operative. Everything about 1664 was expensive, neat.

"And all the time the mother was working here as a counsellor?" 1664 said. "Never mind the father, you'd have thought she would have put a stop to it. I just don't understand how you could let something like that happen. Mind you, I'm so lucky with Bethany. She's very sensible, for a teenager."

Nadine smiled. "Yes, it was a bit ironic about Caroline's job. One of the twins was sectioned in the end. And all because of, you know – the drugs. And it was his brother who got him into it. I wouldn't let my Tom go near either of them. They were ringleaders, a really terrible influence."

"What was he taking, then?" 1664 asked. "I mean, how on earth could you just not notice? Your own child."

"Marijuana, LSD, crack cocaine – everything," Nadine went on. "The mad one attacked someone in the family, too. Of course, he was a danger to himself as well."

25

I fought the urge to dump my lukewarm coffee over Nadine's stupid head.

Ninety per cent of what she'd said was wrong. Herod had never been as much of a chemist as Owen, for example. All Herod did was smoke too much weed: he very rarely even took pills, or that's what Owen told me, anyway. And Herod never attacked anyone. I had no idea where that story came from, but I'd heard it before. People talk a load of shit.

Herod did get sick, though. Really sick.

1664 looked down at the table, her mouth pursed with disapproval. She began tearing the leaflet into strips again. "Oh. Well, that's dreadful but some families bring these things on themselves really, don't they? Sitting back and letting your child live that kind of lifestyle. The mother and father must both be as bad as each other. I'm just glad Bethany's always been so responsible." She sighed. "Especially now."

"Of course," Nadine said.

Silence.

I thought about my father. It was more then two years since I'd seen him. He wouldn't exactly win prizes for being the most amazing dad in the world, but that was no one else's business. I was getting angrier and angrier, listening to that silly cow judging my family.

"Anyway," 1664 said at last, making no sense but filling the quiet. "Anyway."

"Mum?" I heard someone ask. "Can we go in yet? I really want to see Dad."

I looked up and a girl came walking into the canteen wearing the contraceptive St Agnes's uniform – burgundy skirt and blazer, nasty grey socks – but I hardly noticed that. Her black hair was loose around her shoulders, pinned back behind one ear with a blue silk rose. A string of amber beads hung around her neck, just visible behind the unbuttoned collar of her shirt. She was tall for a girl, too. I'd never seen her around. She had to be new in town. Her face was milky white against the black of her hair; she had light brown freckles on her nose and wore no make-up as far as I could tell – but some girls are clever about that, aren't they? I remember Sammy asking his sister why she never wore any and Leila rolling her eyes, saying, "Listen, Sam, the aim's to look as if you're *not* wearing it."

As I sat there, I thought of the other girls I knew: Georgie Hicks with that tidemark of orange make-up halfway down her neck; Gemma Lord's bleached blonde hair and drawn-in eyebrows; Amanda, who was cool but just, well, nothing special. Mousy.

She left them all standing, this tall, pale girl.

I won't have to crick my neck bending to kiss you. The next second, *You've only just seen her. Christ, get a grip.*

But she was looking at me, too.

I don't know how to say it – I felt I'd known her before, that this girl I'd never met in my life was someone I recognised.

It was like looking at my own shadow: she was part of me.

Suddenly, I felt too hot. Then too cold. I looked down at

my hands and they were shaking. Actually shaking.

1664 turned and left with her and it physically hurt, watching her go, as if I'd been kicked in the stomach. 1664 said something to Nadine about a tennis club on the way out but I didn't really hear. I was just looking at the girl as they walked off down the corridor towards the oncology ward. Cancer.

I loved the way she walked, quick and graceful like a dancer.

Shit, I thought. *Shit. I've got to see her again. I've got to find a way of seeing her again.*

I knew, even then. I just knew.

FOUR

"I'm getting the fear," Jono said as we climbed over the first fence into a wide, dark field studded with trees. "This is well creepy."

Bethany rolled her eyes at me. Seemed like she felt the same way about Jono as he did about her.

Jono sat down in the grass, clutching fistfuls of it.

Sammy crouched down beside him. "It's OK, Jon. Come on, we've got to get on site."

"They're coming for us," Jono whispered.

I watched as Bethany knelt at Jono's other side. "It's all right," she said in a soothing voice. "We'll be OK. Let's just get in there and have some beers and a nice sit down."

"No," Jono hissed. "We can't sit down, we can't. Oh, shit."

Bethany patted him on the shoulder. "It's all right," she

said, kindly. "There's really nothing to worry about, is there? We're going to be fine."

And all the time Bethany was talking Jono out of his freak-out, I was thinking, *I don't want her ever to leave. I want her to always be here. She's amazing.* I mean, she didn't even like the guy. It wasn't as if Jono had gone out of his way to be friendly.

At last, Jono got shakily to his feet. Bethany linked arms with him, nodding at me. I took his other arm.

"It's all right, Jono," I told him. "We're going to be fine, man."

"It's cool," Jono said, shrugging us away, standing up on his own. He sounded more like his usual cocky self now. As if it had never happened. "It's all cool."

Bethany shot me a glance, raising one eyebrow slightly. Having a laugh but not rubbing his face in it. I took her by the hand, a silent thank-you.

Sammy took a drag of his rollie and stood surveying the landscape like some kind of explorer down the Amazon. "I reckon the actual fence for the festival is behind those trees. We've just got to get up there and it'll be fine. The security last year was well slack – I remember Dad saying."

It didn't appear that the security this year was slack, but I wasn't about to bring everyone down again. "You're right, that's where the music's coming from. Let's go."

We pegged it across the field and I was pretty pleased with myself; I thought we were doing nicely, all things considered.

Well, I was wrong. We got close, very close, and then there was a bit of a disaster.

I could see the boundary fence through the trees just beyond the next field, a rickety corrugated-iron thing. It was hardly worth the my-job-is-more-important-than-God guys in yellow jackets on the gate.

I laughed. "Let's get in there. I could do with a beer." I grabbed Bethany's hand, feeling her fingers grip mine, warm and dry. A wild burning rush shot through my body as we sped for the trees, peeling ahead of Jono and Sammy. Bethany was fast, especially considering she was running in wellies – not the easiest thing in the world. I could hear her ragged breathing as we sprinted across the tussocky grass and every now and then she would explode into a little fit of giggles, like she couldn't believe what we were doing. I got the impression she'd never done anything like this before – not the breaking-into-a-festival-bit; neither had I – but breaking the rules. She wasn't used to it.

"My mum thinks I'm painting watercolours on the beach!" she gasped, and then, "Jack, what was that?" She stopped suddenly and so did I. Jono and Sammy ran up behind us.

"Guys, it's not a race." Sammy was panting like a dog. He obviously hadn't noticed anything was wrong.

Jono was the next to react – probably still wired with paranoia, despite the tough act. It worked in our favour, though. "Get down!" he hissed and we threw ourselves flat on the ground under trees. As we lay there, slightly damp, I heard voices getting louder, laughter, and faintly in the distance something that sounded like a car engine.

"What's that light?" Sammy whispered. "In the trees?"

"Shut up!" I said. I was trying to think more clearly and get a hold of myself, but I could see it, too: an orangey pulsing glow. Now I could hear branches cracking, more laughter.

"Helloooooo! We know you're theeeeere – we saw you!"

I heard Bethany breathe in sharply.

More crashing. Lurching.

"Yooo-hoooo!"

None of us said a word. By the sound of it, we'd been spotted by a bunch of piss-heads, no doubt also trying to find a gap in the fence: annoying but manageable. But then it got bad. Bethany and I were still holding hands, face down on the ground; the whirring, grinding of a car engine grew louder and the flashing orange lights grew brighter. Then the growling engine stopped, leaving just the pulsing light. It was pretty sinister. I heard the creak of a door opening, the crunch of someone heavy stepping down onto last autumn's dried leaves.

Bethany squeezed my hand tighter. I knew what she must have been thinking: what was the worst that could happen? Being turned over to the cops? Bethany's parents thought she was on a school trip. Talk about blowing your cover. And her dad? Well, he wasn't in hospital any more but I don't think I'd really realized what Bethany was risking till that moment.

"Oh, God," Bethany whispered, so low that I was the only one who heard her. There was an edge of panic in her voice. I grasped her hand a bit tighter, too. She let out a long, steady breath. Taking control. She had guts, always.

Peering through the trees, I saw a Land Rover parked up, more men in fluorescent yellow jackets. Festival security.

"Right, move along, please," I heard one of them call. "Go back to your vehicles. This is a ticketed event and the gate is now closed till eight-thirty tomorrow morning. Come back then." Christ, he sounded like a robot.

"Give us a break, mate!"

"Yeah, come on. It's no skin off of your nose, is it?"

We lay there, silent and still, as an argument broke out between security and the piss-heads. My heart was thudding like mad. What were we going to do if they caught us? OK, so even if they didn't take us to the police, which seemed a bit extreme anyway, I didn't fancy sleeping in some field till the gates opened again. We didn't have tents: Sammy's mum had said we could use the café's dry store as long as we helped out for at least an afternoon – we'd be nice and cosy among the tins of kidney beans and wholemeal burger buns.

We'll just have to lie here till they've gone, I thought, squeezing Bethany's hand again and hoping that mine wasn't starting to sweat. *All we've got to do is stay cool and keep our heads down. It'll be fine. Absolutely fine.*

Then one of the piss-heads started shouting. "Yeah, well, we're not the only ones, are we? If you're going to be a jobsworth, do it properly. There's a load of kids hiding in the trees – just over there."

The bastards had grassed us up.

The argument started again but it was all just a jumble of words to me: adrenalin was surging through my body like boiling tar and I couldn't make any sense of what they were saying.

There was no choice. We couldn't get caught. It was as simple as that.

"Run!" I muttered. "Now! Run for the fence or we're totally shafted."

With Bethany at my side, I got up and pegged it, hoping like hell that Jono and Sammy had the sense to do the same. It was our only chance. I heard footsteps behind us, people shouting. The fence got closer and closer. We sprinted through the trees and slammed into the fence. I heard Sammy yelling, "Here, here! There's a hole!"

He was right – the fence was made of corrugated-iron sheets wired together and mounted on breezeblocks. There was a gap where someone had cut the wiring and lifted open one of the sections like a gate.

One after the other, we squeezed through: Bethany first, then Sammy and Jono. I went last, and those were the long-est thirty seconds of my life. I could almost feel a heavy hand landing on my shoulder, pulling me backwards.

But then I was through and I couldn't hear the guards any more. Had they given up? We stumbled forwards and I knocked over a plastic crate leaning against this old-style gypsy caravan, a proper wooden one with huge wheels and steps going up to the door. We were in some kind of camping field. Someone nearby was playing the guitar. I could hear low voices, music and laughter. Then the night burst open with howling and barking and this massive ball of muscle and teeth hurled itself right at me.

I froze.

What is it they say about dogs? *Show no fear.* Well, I was bricking it but I stood my ground, mainly because I knew Bethany was watching. I didn't want her to think I was a coward.

The dog backed off, snarling – it looked like a Staffy: all fangs and no brains – and I let out a long breath. I felt kind of sorry for him: he'd been left all on his own, chained to the caravan wheel. The others were standing there totally still but as I edged past the Staffy, I saw Bethany smile.

We had escaped. We were in. We had done it.

"Oh, my life," Sammy said. "Oh, my God."

"I never, ever want to do that again," said Jono, not even pretending to be cool, and none of us could stop laughing at him.

And as we walked away from the caravan and the wired dog, this guy stepped down from the back of a Sprinter van with a chimney pipe jammed into the roof. The guitar music had stopped.

Did I know who it was just from the loping, catlike way he moved?

"Are you all right?" he said. "That bloke's a knob. Always going off and leaving his dog on its own. Sends the poor thing mad." His voice was the same; still sounding like he'd just smoked sixty Marlboro Reds and washed them down with a pint of whisky.

I couldn't move; I stood there like an idiot as he walked over.

"What's wrong?" Bethany said, quietly. I drew my hand away from hers. I couldn't hack it, but even so I felt like I'd lost something just by not touching her.

Jono and Sammy said nothing. They knew. They remembered.

Owen. There he was: my brother, the eldest, older than Herod by four and a half minutes. They were eight when I turned up, an attempt to rescue the marriage of our parents (I failed, miserably).

How many years had it been? Five. I'm pretty sure it was five years. I lost track of where he'd gone after India and South America, and so did Mum, I think. He hadn't changed much, though – except his hair was shorter and the dreds were gone, now it just hung dark and ragged around his shoulders. His eyes were always what I remembered. A weird honey colour, tilted. We'd all been stamped with the same eyes: the legacy of a Shoshone woman my great-grand-father married after he stepped off the boat from Ireland and out onto the quay at Ellis Island, New York City.

Owen stood and stared at me a moment: it was a strange feeling, like he was looking through me and seeing some-one else. "What are you doing here?" he said at last, and he laughed. That hadn't changed either – a lazy, sarcastic cackle. "Jesus Christ."

I could have asked him the same thing. I'd spent five years planning what I would say to Owen if I ever saw him again – *Thanks a lot, mate. Now they want* me *to get into Oxford* had been pretty high on the list – but now he was here I couldn't think of anything.

Instead, I ran. I'd been running a lot that night. Maybe I'd just got into the habit.

The others came after me, and as I ran I could still hear Owen laughing. He didn't follow, but then Owen never followed anyone in his life. He was always a leader. A ringleader they used to say.

I stopped at this little stall selling cold beers on the way into the main festival and stumped up the cash for four. They were two quid each as well, but I didn't care. I needed a beer.

We drank in silence and it felt good. Jono and Sammy kept looking at each other, nervous. Bethany had taken my hand again and now I let her. A warm rush of relief washed through me as her fingers gripped mine. It was like the times when you wake up from a bad dream and the panic washes away as you realize your leg hasn't been amputated, or that person hasn't died or whatever.

"Look," I said to them all, lighting a rollie, "it's fine. I'm not going to wig out on you, OK. Let's just pretend that never happened."

Jono shrugged. "Fair enough, mate." Back once again to his usual cocky self, he was grinning and looking around at the strings of fairy lights hanging between stalls, people lurching in and out of these big Indian tents. The smell of weed hovered over everything like some kind of nuclear fall-out cloud. A couple of hard-looking Traveller girls the same age as us were driving pony traps from the car park, laden with stuff people couldn't be bothered to carry to the campsite.

"Are you sure?" Sammy said. "I mean, that's pretty weird, him turning up after all this time—"

"I'm sure."

Bethany said nothing, just lit up a fag and passed it to me, then took my hand in hers again. Our fingers twined together. I was grateful. Most girls would have asked what had just happened, demanded to know, and then wanted to endlessly discuss it. They're such a bunch of psychologists. But not Bethany.

So we went off to the Veggie Café and told a few little white lies to Sammy's mum about how our taxi had got lost in the lanes.

"And we missed the first train as well," Sammy said. "We had to take the slow one."

"Oh for goodness' sake – it stops at every hole in the hedge." Yvonne glanced at her watch. She was wearing a blue and white striped apron over jeans, a long bright pink cardigan covered in tiny mirrors, and a pair of wellies. "But that taxi of yours must have headed halfway to Bristol and back. Didn't you run out of cash?" Yvonne asked. "I hope the driver didn't charge you extra for getting lost." She gave Sammy a long look and he shrugged. Yvonne's no one's fool. If there hadn't been a mile-long queue in the café she might have asked a few more awkward questions.

Bethany smiled. "He did, but there was no point arguing. My mum gave me taxi money, too. So we were fine."

I could see that Sammy was starting to sweat. *Mum asks all these really innocent-sounding questions*, he's said before. *Just kind of tricks things out of you. I can't get anything past her.*

Yvonne looked a bit surprised to see Bethany but, again, she played it cool. "Oh, well that was lucky. I'm Yvonne, by the way."

"This is Bethany," I said, relieved that the questioning seemed to be over. That didn't last long.

"Are you OK, Jack?" Yvonne asked me. "You look like you've seen a ghost."

"I'm just a bit tired," I said.

Yvonne gave me another one of those long looks. "Come and help me a second will you, J? I need to reach a box of teabags from the dry store, and I think you're the only one tall enough. Franky's in the beer tent." She sighed. "Why don't the rest of you all sit down and have a cup of tea, hot chocolate – we've got chai on the go if you fancy it. Sounds like you had a long journey."

When I'd climbed past the tins of beans and packets of

burger buns stashed in the tent next to the kitchen, and finally found the teabags, Yvonne said "Are you OK, Jack?"

"I'm fine, really," I replied. "Just tired, like I said."

She must have felt it was OK to move in for the attack. "I didn't know you had a girlfriend."

"We haven't been together that long."

"Bethany doesn't go to your school, does she? I don't think I've heard Sam mention the name."

I shrugged. "She's at St Agnes's. She's really nice, Yvonne. Really up for helping out, too. I promise."

"I'm sure she's nice. She's very pretty. Natural-looking, unlike most of them nowadays. Bad liar, too." Yvonne shook her head and I flinched. Lucky for Sammy that Yvonne's cool. You really couldn't get anything past her. If she was all uptight and strict about stuff, it'd be a nightmare. "Is Bethany going to be OK with you three boys, though?"

"Yeah," I said, "we'll be fine. Honestly."

Yvonne gave me that look again. "What I mean is, Jack, that I hope you'll be careful. Sensible."

Ugh, God, what was she on about? What did she think I was going to do, lose my virginity in a tent full of baked bean tins with Jono and Sammy as company? Classy.

I nodded, handing her the box of teabags. "Don't worry, Yvonne. We'll be OK."

Just as I said it, the lights went out and someone yelled from the kitchen tent, "Yvonne! The urn and the fridge have gone off, too."

"Bugger," said Yvonne in the darkness. "See you later, Jack. Just don't do anything stupid, will you?"

Then she yelled, "Coming!" I was off the hook.

Bethany and I managed to lose Jono and Sammy outside the cinema tent. There was a little bonfire with hay bales laid out around it and we sat down on one of the bales.

"It's powered by a bike!" Bethany grinned, teeth white in the darkness. "A cinema powered by a bike. Thanks for bringing me, Jack. It's amazing." She passed me the pint of cider we were sharing, taking a long draw from a joint. But then the smile disappeared and she stared down at the ground, already scattered with plastic pint glasses and greasy paper plates. It was meant to be a green festival but that didn't seem to have stopped everyone chucking stuff all over the place. "I was really scared, you know," she said quietly. "When we nearly got caught, I was terrified."

I smiled at her. "It's all right. Me too. Only a bullshitter like Jono would pretend they weren't."

She passed me the joint, blowing out a long coil of smoke, staring out at the mayhem unfolding around us. "If Mum finds out I'm here, she'll go mental. She'll go on and on about how I shouldn't upset Dad and she's right." Bethany shut her eyes a moment. "I don't know how she does it but she can make me feel … worse than anything. So guilty."

At first, I didn't know what to say.

"Listen," I told her eventually, gripping her hand. "We're

here now. It's like we're walking on a tightrope between two skyscrapers. We can't look down. Even if we do get caught – which we won't – what's the point if we haven't had a good time, OK? So don't think about it. And anyway, you deserve a break. Your dad's been really ill – you've moved house, gone to a new school. It's a nightmare. Have some fun."

I passed back the joint. Bethany smiled uncertainly but said, "You're right." She shrugged. "Jesus, I thought it was bad enough when Mum and Dad said we had to leave London because of his job." She shut her eyes.

For a moment we just sat there, holding hands, her fingers squeezing mine. What could I say to her? *Don't worry, everything's going to be all right?* I don't make promises I can't keep.

"Thanks for coming." I kissed her again; we both tasted of tobacco, burnt weed. I probably shouldn't have even been smoking the stuff. Maybe I had the same switch in my brain that Herod did. A switch just waiting to be flipped, opening a door to strange places. Letting the Creature in.

Stop it, I told myself. *Stop thinking about that.*

The psychiatrist said it was most likely Herod's gigantic skunk habit that had scrambled his mind, along with what he called "the pressures of late adolescence", and there I was anyway, smoking Buggy's sticky like there'd be no tomorrow. A gambling man.

"Jack," Bethany said "Are you OK? You were miles away. I'm not going to go on about this or anything, but who was that guy outside the caravan? Don't say if you don't want to."

I watched as a crowd of girls stumbled by, faces painted with glitter that shone in the firelight. An old hippy with a beard walked past wearing a tutu and a top hat, smoking a pipe, arm in arm with a lady who had long grey plaits down to her waist.

"He's my brother," I said. "Owen. He left." I didn't really want to think about it, to be honest.

Bethany waited, edging slightly closer. The night was getting chilly, and we wrapped our arms around each other's shoulders, close together. She was a good listener. Didn't force stuff out of you. Just waited.

"I haven't seen him for five years."

"Oh," said Bethany, and gripped my hand in hers. I loved that about her, the way she just let me talk, not pushing.

I've been pressured into talking about private stuff too many times. I'm sick of it.

"But don't you want to find Owen now you're both here?" Bethany asked after a while. She didn't say anything about why he'd gone: it was as if she just knew not to go there. "Five years is like, wow, a long time."

Owen. I couldn't believe I'd actually seen him.

I wondered if Bethany's mum had passed on the gossip-version of Herod and Owen's story – all that bullshit about crack she'd heard in the hospital

I shook my head. "What would I have to say to him? Mum was gutted when she realized he was never going to

43

bother with uni. First of all he kept saying he'd deferred. But it never came to anything. He'd got into Oxford, too. Now all Mum goes on about is me getting ridiculously good marks in everything."

"So you're meant to do what Owen didn't. That's a load of crap. Honestly." Bethany shrugged. "What about your dad? What's he like about it?"

"He's not around."

She didn't go there, either. Good move.

Bethany just accepted what I told her, without asking too much. Still, I couldn't help feeling like I'd given away a piece of myself, even though it was just a fragment of the story. I hadn't told her why Owen left, had I? Was that how she'd felt talking about her dad, that she was giving too much away? I'll always remember the look she gave me on the train – so *grateful*.

It isn't your fault, I'd told her.

Bethany passed me the cider. I finished it and was about to chuck the plastic pint glass away when I remembered what she was like with her fag ends.

"Come on." I grinned at her. Bethany had risked a lot for this. "Let's find a bin and another pint."

FIVE

Bethany and me stumbled around the site, drinking and laughing and smoking, hand in hand. I couldn't believe my luck: that I was there with her. Even so, my mind kept wandering down some pretty strange pathways, as if seeing Owen had unlocked doors kept shut for years. Or maybe it was Bethany, and the way I felt like I could tell her anything. Either way I thought about stuff probably best forgotten; I couldn't seem to stop myself. It was like going back in time – I could see it all so clearly.

I'm sitting in the doorway of the shed at the bottom of our back garden. There's nothing on TV so I'm watching Herod work instead. He's meant to be doing pottery coursework, but Herod is an artist. He would be doing this even if school didn't make him.

I'm not sure if he minds me sitting on the step, or if he just hasn't noticed I'm even here. It's late on Sunday afternoon. Light slants across the tangled garden. Mum and Louis have had friends over for lunch: I can just hear their laughter drifting down through the mess of flowers and overgrown bushes, the clink of wine glasses too.

Herod is standing at the workbench where, in the spring, Mum sows lettuce seeds in trays and pokes tiny tomato plants into pots of compost. With total calm and patience, Herod is turning a lump of pale grey clay into a rose. All this takes place inside a plastic salad bowl. He uses damp sponges to prop up the petals as they are formed, keeping them from squashing against the sides of the bowl. His fingers move fast, then slow again, patting, pressing, stroking. The rose is about the size of a football, and perfect – each petal is really growing, unfolding from the tight hard bud of clay. It is as if some bright, hot part of Herod himself passes through his grey-stained fingertips into the clay, bringing it to life.

Every few minutes, Herod pauses, picks up a roll-up from the terracotta plant pot he is using as an ash tray and takes a draw, breathing out a cloud of sickly sweet smoke – it's one of the kind he makes himself. I think it might be weed, the stuff Mum and Louis' friends smoke around the kitchen table late at night when they've drunk a lot of wine and they think I'm asleep in bed. Sometimes Herod takes a swig from the cup of tea Mum got me to bring out half an hour ago: I don't even think he realizes it's cold. He missed lunch but Mum knows as well as I do that Herod won't eat till this is finished. When his work is over for the day, Herod will walk into the kitchen, boil a pan of pasta and eat a huge plate of it with cheese and ketchup, then drink two cans of Coke from the fridge and fall asleep on the sofa for an hour.

"Oh, well," Mum said last time. "At least he can cook. Well, sort of."

"She's done it again. Bitch."

I turn and here is Owen, his hair wet from the shower. He's got a couple of dreadlocks and beads of water cling to them.

I think he stayed at someone else's house last night. He came in through the front door early this morning when I was the only one up, watching Herod's *Lost Boys* video. Owen slumped down next to me and watched till the end. His face looked all weird – his jaw kept kind of jumping and twitching.

After a moment, Herod looks up, wiping his hands on his jeans. A frown crosses his face but clears when he sees it's Owen. "What?"

"Dad. Next weekend. It's not happening."

Sadness crashes through me: it's like being hit in the belly with a football. I haven't seen Dad since before I was eight and I'm almost ten. We were meant to be going to London to see him. My eyes feel all hot but I'm not going to cry, so I stare down at my hands, dusty with dried clay. Herod gave me a piece to play with when I brought the tea but I couldn't make it do what I wanted, so now it sits at my side – a dried-up lump of earth.

I'm so angry. I've been looking forward to London for ages, spent hours imagining what it will be like to see my dad again. And then there's all the cool stuff from America he promised he'd bring: Levis, loads of Oreo cookies. Now it's all ruined. This is not fair.

"Why?" Herod asks, simply. He takes another swig of tea, swallows, pulls a face and ditches the rest out of the door; Owen ducks out of the way, moving faster than a cat. Herod's out of his trance now. Noticing things, like cold tea.

"A bullshit excuse about next week. From her, not him." Owen frowns, and I know that when Mum and Louis' friends have gone, there will be another argument.

Herod shrugs and turns back to his clay. "I don't really blame her," he says, "after what he did."

"She needs to get over that," Owen replies, leaning over me to pick up Herod's joint. He relights it, sitting on the step next to me, taking a long drag. "It's her problem, not ours. Poor Jack," he says, patting me on the head like a dog. I don't mind. "You're going to be so royally fucked up by this."

"Why don't we just go anyway?" I say. "Mum doesn't have to know. We could lie – make something up. She'll believe Herod."

Owen and Herod both turn to stare at me. And Owen laughs.

* * *

I didn't see Owen again that night after Bethany and me left the cinema tent, although I can't deny that I couldn't help scanning faces in the crowd, looking over the little groups of people sitting around in the café, wondering if he'd be there. But he never was. If Jono and Sammy hadn't seen Owen, too, perhaps I would have convinced myself that I'd imagined the whole thing.

We had a good one, though – Jono, Sammy, Bethany and I. Drank too much cider, smoked a lot of Buggy the Dealer's lovely sticky. I think everyone threw up at least once and Sammy chucked a proper whitey. We worked for Yvonne the graveyard shift on Saturday night (midnight till six) and it was a laugh – frying up veggie burgers in a massive industrial-sized pan, mixing salad in plastic crates, cutting up banana bread, making salad dressing, laughing at the casualties who came lurching in at three in the morning. Even Jono and Bethany seemed to be getting on OK, which I was relieved about because at first that had worried me a bit; I thought Jono might get embarrassed that Bethany had been the one who talked him down from the fear and start acting like even more of a prat than usual.

Sometime before four, Sammy and Jono went off to buy more Rizlas, so for a while it was just me and Bethany, working together like a machine. We were a team; again, I felt like I'd known her for years and years. We hardly spoke, didn't need to. She didn't say anything else about Owen: she didn't try to pry. I'd told her and that was it. At five o'clock Sammy returned to donate a pint of cider, guilt-ridden and off his face. Bethany and I swigged the cider, chopped tomatoes, unwrapped huge slabs of cake and cut them up, plunged endless jugs of coffee. As the night tipped towards morning, the burger orders dried up and we sold acres of banana bread and endless cups of tea to people with the munchies.

At half-past five, Sammy's sister Leila came in with some of her friends. I used to quite fancy Leila, obviously knowing that I didn't have a chance, considering that she's twenty-one and really hot, just out of uni.

"Jesus, Jack," she said, leaning on the bar. She'd let her hair grow into an Afro and painted silver streaks through it. "Are you OK? I saw Sammy and Jon over by the cinema. They're absolutely munted, but he said you and your girl-friend had it all under control."

Cheeky bastards. My girlfriend, though; my girlfriend. I grinned. "We're all right," I said. "Bit knackered."

And then Leila leaned closer and said, "I'm not sure if I… Listen, Jack, I saw your brother. Owen. Did you know he was here?"

Damn. I could deal with Owen when I was pretty much the only one who'd seen him – then I could forget about it. But Sammy's family knew too much about mine. What if Yvonne had seen Owen? What if she called Mum to tell her? The chances of Yvonne not mentioning me were too small to think about.

I shrugged. "Yeah, I've seen him already." I smiled at her, turning on the charm. "Listen, Leila, all this is a bit kind of complicated."

Leila nodded. "OK." I think she guessed I wasn't really meant to be there. "I won't say anything to Mum and Dad. Take care, anyway. Sam owes you one."

I didn't think so. Sammy and Jono might have landed us in it, but they had given me a gift: a full two hours with Bethany. When six o'clock came and a load of students turned up to take over for the breakfast shift, Bethany turned to me and smiled, saying, "Come on. Come with me."

We walked out into the grey light hand in hand.

We slept beneath a willow tree, wrapped in Yvonne's picnic blanket, holding each other, and I don't know why the Dream had to come back that night, when I was with Bethany. It's not really a dream, either, that's the wrong word because it actually happened. It's just that sometimes it happens again while I'm sleeping: I go to another place, another time, but always the same moment.

I'm walking up the stairs but I'm not going to make it in time—

I sat up, shivering, sucking in great gasps of cold air. Outside somewhere. On the grass. Not there any more. As always, it took me a moment to remember. Someone was calling my name.

"Jack," Bethany said. "Jack, what's wrong? You're shaking. Are you cold?"

She had the sense not to touch me. Instead she just sat at my side, drawing the picnic blanket closer. How did she know not to touch me – that I would freak out if she laid a finger on me? Mum found that out the hard way, the first time this happened. But Bethany just knew. My whole body was shuddering as if I'd been electrocuted: fingertips, knees, shoulders. I couldn't stop. My back was cold with sweat. I had to concentrate on breathing or I would have just stopped.

It's OK, I told myself. *You got there in time. You made it.*

I couldn't look at her, just stared straight ahead. At last, the shaking ended. A tree root dug into my leg. I moved. Must have been about eight in the morning. A group of guys walked by, holding beers, arms slung around each other.

"Sorry," I said. "Just a dream." I knew that sounded ridiculous considering the state I was in, like saying a gale that ripped the tops off garden sheds and sent trees crashing through people's greenhouses was nothing but a shower of rain.

Bethany lit a cigarette and passed it to me. "A bad dream. It's OK," she said. Not asking any questions. Amazing. At last, she rested her hand on my knee, warm, bringing me back into the world, away from it all. Away from the Creature, and what it did to Herod.

* * *

"What were you dreaming about, Jack?" said the counsellor (not mum, obviously, they had to get someone else in), a woman with hair dyed an unlikely red, and too many silver rings squeezed on to fat fingers. The rings bothered me; her fingers looked as if they were going to fall off like lambs' tails when they've been docked. "It must have been a bad dream. You pushed your mother really hard when she tried to wake you, didn't you? Do you want to tell me about it? It might make things better."

I said nothing, just stared out of the window. I could see our car parked outside, beneath a tree shedding its leaves.

The counsellor pushed a pile of blank paper towards me, some coloured pencils. "Some people find it helpful to draw what they see in their dreams," she said. "Try it if you like."

How old does she think I am? Five? I wondered. I stared out of the window and said nothing.

I felt as though Bethany could see right through me, that somehow she just knew.

I didn't mind.

SIX

We arrived back in town victorious. When Jono, Sammy, Bethany and I all parted in the park on Sunday afternoon in the rain, we even had a group hug. God, it had been good. We were all high with delight.

Bethany smiled at Jono and Sammy, wheeling her bike. I was amazed it hadn't been nicked, locked up at the station all weekend. "Thanks so much for letting me come with you," she said. "I loved it."

Jono shrugged and muttered, "It's not as if we had much choice." But then he flipped open a pack of Lucky Strikes and offered her the second-to-last one before lighting up himself, so I knew he was over it. He'd accepted her.

"No worries," Sammy said. "Mum was well impressed. She'll probably be up for letting you and Jack work at Glastonbury." He laughed. "Not sure about me and Jono, though. We did slack off a bit, to be fair."

"Glastonbury," Bethany said. "That would be amazing." But then her smile disappeared and I knew she was thinking about her dad.

I squeezed her hand tighter. "We'll definitely be there," I said. "Will you be all right getting home? Shall I walk you?"

Bethany shook her head, smiling. "It's too far. I'll be OK on my bike."

I took her hand and we walked away from the others, kissing beneath the tall dark trees, her bike propped between us. I could have stayed for hours but she pulled away.

"I'll phone you," she called over her shoulder, black hair flying out like a flag as she pedalled away. "Bye, Jack."

I thought we were so unstoppable. I thought this would never end.

I didn't go straight home. Mum and Louis were in France till Wednesday and once Bethany had ridden off across the park, I felt kind of hollow and depressed.

"Come back to mine," Sammy said. "We'll watch a film."

Jono yawned and said his mum would have dinner ready soon and sloped off across the park in the opposite direction from Bethany.

So it was about half eight by the time I reached the top of our street. Even from there, I could see the sitting-room light was on, a yellow glow against the light evening sky of mid-summer.

This could only mean one thing: Mum and Louis were back early. For a moment, I had this spooky, shivery feeling that maybe Owen had come home, but I pushed that away. He wouldn't. He was in the country again, there was no denying that, but I knew there was still some action at the festival – it didn't officially close till Monday morning. Owen was never the kind to leave a party early. No, if the lights were on, my parents were back. The question was, how long had they been home for? If it was only a couple of hours, I'd be fine. Any longer and things might be sticky.

They were sticky.

When I got in I closed the door behind me, super quietly. I'm good at that. I stood in the hallway, listening. Mum's brown leather handbag was hanging over the banister at the bottom of the stairs. The faint scent of one of Louis' Gauloises drifted through from the sitting room, and with it came a muddle of voices, some of which I didn't recognize. And some of which I did. I heard Mum and Louis. And I heard Bethany.

Something had gone wrong, badly, but they still didn't know I was here. *I could leg it now*, I thought. *Come back later when the fallout's less intense.* But Bethany was in there. I wasn't about to leave her to ride this out on her own.

We'd been found out.

I went in. Bethany was sitting on the sofa between 1664 – wearing expensive clothes and an expression that would kill a rat – and a bald-headed man with dark circles beneath his eyes. His face was narrow, clever-looking. Bethany's dad. You could tell straight away how sick he'd been. He was so thin, and he had the far-off expression in his eyes of a traveller, someone who has seen places you can't even imagine.

Bethany looked at me; I looked at her. She was still in her pink dress, but the green coat had been replaced with a huge, tasselled cardigan, the wellies with cowboy boots. Even then, I wanted to hold her.

Mum was in the armchair, Louis leaning against the back of it. It wasn't Louis who was smoking: it was Mum. She hadn't touched one for nearly four years. Why the hell had they come back from France early? There was something else going on, something bigger than the nasty little drama in our sitting room.

Louis broke the silence. "Jack?"

Bethany shook her head, very slightly. *Let them do the talking.* I knew exactly what she was trying to tell me.

Mum turned to look at me. A strand of her sandy, curly hair had escaped from its ponytail and she tucked it behind her ear. When she spoke I knew instantly that she was furious but not with me. Bit of a surprise, considering. Then who?

"Bethany's parents would like us to tell you not to see her again," she said.

I stared past them all, my eyes meeting Bethany's. No way. I hadn't even met her stupid parents yet. Bethany's eyes had that hot, burning look again. Was she going to cry?

I thought of not seeing her tomorrow, and the day after that, or the day after that, for ever, and I started to panic; it was like the walls of the room were closing in on me.

"No! You can't do that." The words spewed out of my mouth before I could stop myself. "You don't understand!"

"Mum, *please*," Bethany whispered, frantically. "I'm sorry I lied to you about the festival, but that wasn't Jack's fault—"

"I've heard enough, thank you," 1664 snapped. She turned, giving me absolute daggers. "Luckily, Bethany's friend's mother was responsible enough to tell us about your little jaunt." It was a dig at Mum, hinting that she'd known about the festival and gone along with it.

Mands' cousin from the girls' school – Amelia – she must have blabbed to someone about what we'd been up to.

I turned to Mum. "Come on, this isn't fair," I said, trying to keep my voice calm, steady. "I know I should have asked about the festival, too, but—"

Mum just shook her head, silently telling me to shut up.

"I'd like your assurance, Caroline, that your son won't be bothering my daughter again," said 1664.

Bothering her daughter? Like I was some kind of creepy stalker. *Pompous bitch!* I couldn't believe this was actually happening.

"After all," 1664 went on, "I'm sure you'll understand that

58

I don't want Bethany involved in drugs after what happened to your poor son. I don't want her mixed up with mental illness."

You could have heard a feather drop.

"Angela," Bethany's dad said, quietly, "that's none of our business."

"Well, I think it is our business at the moment," 1664 said, voice tight and angry. "Unfortunately."

Bethany put both hands over her mouth, blatantly horrified at her mother's stupid, big mouth. So she did know, then – about Herod – and in that horrible moment I loved her all the more because she hadn't said a word to me about it.

It's true, I thought. *That's what this is – I love her. I love her.*

I looked up; she was watching me. Our eyes locked together. She felt the same. I knew it. I wanted to run across the room and hold her; I wanted to never let go.

And now it was all coming to an end.

Mum put down her cigarette, letting it rest in the ashtray on the windowsill. Her hand was shaking slightly. I could tell she was really angry but holding it in, trying to be reasonable: far scarier than someone just letting rip.

"Jack is not a drug user." She spoke in this awful, calm voice. "And I'm not sure if you realize, Angela, that mental illness isn't actually contagious."

Bethany's mum was looking confused now, embarrassed. "That – that's not what I meant."

"And even if Jack were using," Mum went on, "I would hope that he trusted us enough to ask for help."

OK, so I felt pretty guilty then. Everyone was quiet. No one dared interrupt.

"Let me tell you," Mum said, "the worst thing is when your child is suffering and they don't come to you. Believe me, that's when you really blame yourself."

A thick, nasty silence stretched on.

Bethany started to cry, silently. Tears streamed down her face.

"I think you'd better go now, Mr and Mrs Jones," Louis said, quietly.

1664 looked away, sharply, staring blankly out of the window.

"Of course," Bethany's dad said. "We should go. I'm sorry to have intruded on your evening." He did look properly ill. Really tired, as if every movement was a massive effort. He smiled at me. "Listen, Jack, I know this is hard to accept, but we feel that as Beth just started a new school last term, she really needs to concentrate on her GCSEs at the moment. You'll all be going into Year Eleven in September." He got to his feet, leaning heavily on the chair. He patted her on the shoulder. "We'll leave you to it. I really am sorry about all this." You could tell he meant what he'd said.

I watched in a kind of daze as they herded her out of the door. Bethany turned to me. She looked paler than ever; her eyes were dark holes. I've never seen anyone look so scared.

If her dad died, she'd be left with no one but her mother. I saw it in her face, clear as if she'd just told me. And then, the next second, I saw something else: defiance. They weren't going to stop us. They couldn't. I made myself smile, standing there in the middle of all this. I smiled at her so she knew I wouldn't let her down.

The front door closed with a click, leaving behind a sickly cloud of Angela's perfume.

"Idiot woman," Louis said, quietly, as if to himself. "Honestly, you'd think they'd want the girl to make friends in a new town, not shut her away."

Mum turned to me. Oh, God, she was pissed off but so was I.

"But they're not just friends, are they? Jack, what is going on?" she demanded.

"I like her, OK?" I shouted. "I met her at a party and she's my girlfriend. I don't have to tell you everything. How could you just let them do that? What century do you think we're living in?"

"Oh, shut up!" Mum sounded exhausted. "What did you think you were doing, going off to a festival with a young girl you hardly know without even asking our permission?"

"I'm really sorry, OK. I just wanted to go, and I was afraid you'd say no. There was no harm in it."

"No harm in it?" Mum snapped. "Oh, clearly not, Jack. It's all absolutely fine, isn't it?"

"You can't stop us seeing each other."

"Don't you dare try me," Mum snapped.

"Look," said Louis, "if it's not what Bethany's parents want, we have to respect that."

"But it's so unfair—"

Mum cut in on me. "Listen, Jack, are you smoking? Were you taking anything this weekend?"

"No!" I yelled. "How many times do I have to tell you I'm not Herod? I'm not Owen, OK? Just because they fucked up doesn't mean I will. Jesus Christ!"

All right, so I was lying a little bit but she was so paranoid it was ridiculous.

"Don't swear at your mother," Louis said. Both of us ignored him.

"You don't know what might happen," Mum said, quietly. "Owen was fine. Herod wasn't. How am I supposed to trust you if you sneak around like this? Trust is a two-way process, Jack."

Silently, I cursed myself. I should have taken the chance and asked them about the festival. It had just seemed so much easier not to bother, especially when I thought they were both going to be safely in France the entire weekend.

Mum shook her head. She wasn't finished yet. "And Bethany's father's obviously really unwell – he obviously doesn't need this kind of upset. What's wrong with you? My God, Jack." Then, to my horror, Mum started crying. Huge sobs that shook her body. Louis hugged her but she didn't stop.

"I'm really sorry," I said, automatically. Did I feel guilty then or what? She was really upset.

Louis shook his head, irritated. "You should have asked us. Since when did we become so unreasonable that you can't tell us what you're doing?"

"Anyway, Jack," Mum said, "you're grounded for the whole summer. No television, either."

I didn't take much notice. Mum's always saying over the top stuff and then forgetting about it once she's calmed down.

Almost as an afterthought, she turned to me and said, "I didn't even you know had a girlfriend." She shook her head. "Sometimes I feel you don't tell me anything at all. I don't know what's wrong with you at the moment."

Oh, no. We weren't going to take that particular conversational path. Not if I could help it. I'd rather she yelled at me. Anything but, *Darling, you know that I'm always here to talk, don't you?* Brings me out in the cold chills every time; it's no picnic having a counsellor for your mother.

Time to change the subject. "Mum," I said, "what's going on? Something's happened, hasn't it? I thought you weren't coming back till Wednesday."

Louis gave me one of his sarcastic looks. "That much is clear." He and Mum looked at each other for a moment.

"Its Herod," she said. "His friend Andrea from the Peace Centre called Louis' mother in Paris. We gave the Centre Sabine's number as an emergency contact in case anyone ever needed to speak to us and no one was here. Herod's gone. He's left the Centre. Possibly he's even left Dorset."

"No one knows where he is," Louis said. "That's why Andrea was so worried. Apparently she was very upset on the telephone, very shaken."

So that was it. Herod was missing.

Mum glanced out of the window, as if she could just turn around and Herod would be standing there. She swallowed before speaking, struggling to spit out the words: "We've called the police, of course. The local force down there. They searched the whole house and all the parkland around it, but he just wasn't anywhere…" She paused. "The policewoman said we wouldn't believe how many people are found hiding in their own homes – just wanting to get away from things. She said sometimes they don't want to be found and we had to be ready because if that was Herod's choice there was nothing anyone could do." She turned back to Louis. "But last time we saw him Herod didn't seem like that at all, did he? Wanting to get away?"

Louis shrugged, rubbing her shoulder. "I don't know. I didn't think so."

"Oh, God," Mum said. "I'm going to have to phone Edward. He ought to know, at least."

"I wouldn't bother calling Dad," I said, quietly. "It's not as if there's much point."

"Jack—" Louis began, but Mum was properly crying now and he turned to her instead.

I felt numb, frozen. They didn't need to say any more.

It was pretty obvious why they'd come rushing back across the Channel.

Then the phone rang and everyone jumped. I was the first to reach it. "Hello?"

I recognized the caller's voice straight away: sixty Marlboro Reds, a pint of whisky. "Jack." Owen laughed, lazy, sarcastic. "Wait. Don't hang up. Turns out you left just in time. Pissing it down here. We're in the pub. So tell them we're coming. Probably tomorrow." I knew he was smiling. "It's time I got home for a visit." The line went dead just as Mum yanked the phone out of my hand, glaring at me.

"What's the matter with you?" she snapped, for the second time.

"It wasn't Herod," I snapped back. I waited a minute, can't deny I enjoyed keeping them in suspense. "It was Owen. He's coming home."

I turned and went out into the hall, letting the door slam behind me, leaving Mum and Louis alone and speechless. In the kitchen I stood by the fridge a moment, holding on to the open door, staring in at an ancient Parmesan rind and a gnarled slice of melon.

Get a grip, I told myself, drinking milk straight from the bottle. I was starving. All I could think of was Herod and the Creature. I knew I needed to steer my mind away from all that. I had a sudden memory of sailing with Dad one time when we visited him in San Francisco – the only time. He'd borrowed a boat from a friend, the kind with two hulls

– a catamaran. I remember Dad leaning on the rudder so we slid past a slimy green rock sticking out of the sea, salt water in my face, steering us away. He was like a superhero, I thought. There was nothing he couldn't do. Except call us more than once every six months. No, he didn't seem able to do that.

Thinking too much about Herod and the Creature was a mental danger zone. Thinking about Dad wasn't much better.

But worst of all, Bethany wasn't there.

I was absolutely screwed.

I had to have more.

SEVEN

After supper I lay on my bed listening to Radiohead. The music wasn't enough. I was tired to the bone – Bethany and I had worked all night, catching only a few hours' rest after dawn – but even so, I knew sleep wasn't going to come easily that night. I saw her every time I closed my eyes, black hair falling across her face, the silver spider brooch on her coat.

I turned the stereo off, lay in silence, staring up into the shadows. Years ago, when I was a kid, I'd stuck glow-in-the-dark stars on the ceiling. No, Herod had done it for me, arranging them carefully into galaxies and solar systems. I'd never got around to taking them off.

I opened the window and leaned out to smoke a fag, but the itch didn't go away: I didn't really want to smoke.

I wanted Bethany.

I couldn't have her.

That's what they reckon, I thought, remembering the look on Bethany's face as she left. I smiled to myself in the lamplight.

Downstairs, in the room below – Louis' study – I could hear Mum's voice. She was speaking to someone on the telephone. "Edward, he's not a child any more. Of course I've called the police— Yes, yes— But we don't know he's actually unwell."

She was talking to my dad about Herod and it sounded like he was worried, which surprised me. Hypocrite. *If you care that much*, I thought, *why don't you call more often? Why don't you come and visit?*

Mum had called the police. Somehow, hearing that again made the whole thing seem more real. Herod was gone: officially a missing person.

I wondered if she'd mention Owen and I found myself thinking about that disaster of a trip to London.

"We shouldn't be taking him," Owen said to Herod. Then he turned to me. "Come on, Jack, just go home, OK? How many times do we have to ask?"

We were at the train station. I'd followed them out of the house, uninvited, whilst Mum and Louis were at a garden centre.

"Don't treat me like a baby. I said we should come." What if Dad had gone by the time we found his hotel? I was scared, but I wasn't about to admit that to either of them. What if they just went to London without me?

"Shut up. Two day returns to Paddington." Owen handed over the money to the cashier, a bored-looking old woman in glasses.

"It was my idea," I repeated. "Listen, if you don't take me, I'll tell."

"You're a devious little bastard, aren't you?" Owen sighed, glancing at Herod.

"He's right, though. It was his idea." Herod said.

Owen turned back to the cashier. "Child's day return, too, please."

Owen and Herod went everywhere together. They were always doing stuff that I was loads too young for. This time, I was part of it. I couldn't stop myself grinning as we crossed the platform and got onto our train.

We found four seats together. Owen lit a cigarette the moment we sat down. "Listen," he said, "here's the rules: no running off, no whining and no talking. Got it?"

"Yes," I told him. "Definitely."

I was going to see my dad. I would have done anything.

Shame it didn't work out how I'd hoped.

We found the hotel in a square of tall white houses with iron railings outside, all facing onto a garden. The warm rich smell of roses hung everywhere. Even the stink of car exhaust fumes had faded and we were only ten minutes' walk from the nearest Tube stop. I watched a woman with glossy blonde hair step out of a black cab in front of a house on the far side of the square. It was so quiet here the click of her heels on the pavement echoed faintly.

"That's it," Owen said. "Where that woman just went. That's the hotel."

Herod frowned, very slightly. I followed him and Owen across the street. I remember feeling a bit let down – this wasn't what I had expected at all. I knew my dad was rich. Mum had told me he was incredibly clever, that the computer software he designed was like nothing anybody had seen before and that it was making him a lot of money. So shouldn't he be staying in some swanky place like you see in films, with a red carpet outside and uniformed flunkies at the door?

"Christ, this looks expensive," Owen said cheerfully as we climbed the chalk-white steps. Tiny green bushes in clay pots sat on each step. The front door was painted glossy black. I didn't know how Owen had figured out where to go – there wasn't even a sign outside saying it was a hotel.

The entrance hall was a blur of golden floorboards, white walls, an antique desk, flowers in enormous vases taller than me. Sunlight shone in through a crack in the blinds; a chandelier cast its shimmering reflection on the high ceiling.

"Excuse me?" The receptionist's voice was icy. "This is a private—" She stared at us, her eyes passing over me and practically bulging with horror as they rested on Owen and Herod. Owen had dreds then and both of them looked like proper crusties with knackered old jeans, big boots. Owen was wearing a Rage Against the Machine T-shirt and Herod had a safety pin through one ear at the time. "… it's a private hotel," the receptionist finished, weakly.

"Good," Owen said, cheerfully. "We're looking for Edward MacNamara. Is he still here?"

The receptionist raised one eyebrow. Her face was so perfect, like it had been painted on. She frowned, looking at us as if we stank. "I'm sorry, but I'm afraid we can't give out our guests' details. Who are you?"

"He's our dad," I said. "We've come to see him. Please." I was eight years old.

For a few seconds, everyone stared. Owen said afterwards that if it hadn't been for me they would never have got past the receptionist.

She picked up her telephone.

I focused on the lift (screened off behind a wrought-iron gate), waiting for Dad to appear, but five minutes later, a door next to the receptionist's desk opened on silent hinges and my dad walked in; he'd taken the stairs.

He was tall and suntanned, out of place on a grey day in London. It was like looking at an older, darker version of Owen and Herod – some kind of photocopy. Creepy. The same high cheekbones, the same yellow cat's eyes. Black hair, eyebrows like ticks drawn in charcoal.

"What the hell are you doing here?" Dad said. He was wearing a blue suit but it was as if he were dressing up.

I could tell he didn't normally look that smart. I noticed a worn leather bracelet on his wrist, and he had a silver earring, too. I don't think he even saw me at first, just the twins.

"Hi, Dad," Owen said, unsmiling.

Herod kept quiet, hands in pockets. He looked kind of edgy, though, shoulders hunched, staring at the polished wooden floorboards.

"Does your mother know you're here?" said Dad. "What the hell's going on?"

"We came to see you," Owen said, simply.

I glanced at Herod. He stared straight ahead and said, "No. No."

It didn't make any sense. Dad and Owen both turned to him a moment, each wearing matching expressions of confusion. I came to know that look of Herod's very well – it was a kind of emptiness spreading across his face, like the real Herod had drained away, leaving something else that only used his face as a mask.

And then Dad saw me.

I had been waiting for this moment for almost two years.

"Jesus Christ, Owen." Dad's voice was steady and calm now but you could tell he was really angry. "What's the meaning of this? Your mother is not going to be happy."

Owen just shrugged.

At that moment, the wrought-iron gate moved silently to one side, the lift door opened and out stepped the blonde woman we'd seen in the street. She was younger than Dad and wore a grey suit with high-heeled shoes. I remember noticing her fingernails for some reason – they were shiny and pink like the inside of a shell.

"Edward?" she said. "Is everything all right?"

"Jessica!" Now Dad sounded properly annoyed, not just icy calm.

She opened her handbag, took out a packet of cigarettes and lit one. "Never mind, Edward – I can see you're busy." The door to the street closed after her with a click, letting in a gust of warm air.

I remember the silence. Wanting it to be over. Even I could see we'd made a massive mistake.

"Listen," Dad said, "all of you. I have a meeting this afternoon. It's not just any old meeting. I'm going to see one of the guys who founded Apple about some software. You know, the computer company. I can't cancel it. I'm literally about to leave. My flight's at eight this evening and I'm heading straight to the airport after the meeting. You're going to have to go home. I'm sorry."

"Right," Owen replied. "Right. We should have called your secretary to arrange an appointment."

The receptionist had been pretending to ignore us but she flinched when Owen said that.

Dad's eyes narrowed. "Well, you shouldn't have done this." He jerked his head at me, then turned his back on the twins and crouched down at my side so I was now taller than him. "Jack," he said, "I'm really sorry. I want to see you very much. I really do. But it just can't be now. I'll fix something up with your mother, OK? I promise."

He reached out to pat my shoulder, but I pulled away.

We stood there in silence. *You could change your flight*, I kept thinking. *You could buy another ticket, like on the train.*

But Dad didn't change his flight. He just ordered us a taxi.

He gave me a hug, but Owen and Herod stepped away from him, moving as if they were one person. They'd disappeared into their own world. Twins.

"Goodbye," Dad said. "I'll sort something out soon, I promise."

"Bye." It came out in a whisper. I was afraid I might cry.

Herod and Owen said nothing.

"Take care, Jack, won't you? All of you." Dad turned and walked away, very quickly.

We were meant to be taken home in a car summoned up by the receptionist, but Owen talked the driver into dropping us off at Paddington station. We hadn't even discussed it, but none of us wanted to be chauffeured out of the way. We were going to retreat with dignity, at least.

When we were on the train, Owen was the first to speak. "He must be loaded now. A five-hour round-trip taxi ride? And that hotel. Jesus Christ."

Herod had been gazing out of the window, fiddling with the zip on his hoodie. Now he turned and stared at us.

"We never take anything from him ever again." Even Owen looked surprised at the tone of his voice. "Not a fucking penny, OK?" Herod said.

Owen stared at him. "All right. OK. OK."

It was a pact.

I can still see the moment we realized that Herod was truly, properly ill. Mum, Louis and I were in the kitchen one Sunday night, eating spaghetti carbonara. Owen had gone out somewhere.

The door swung open and Herod came in. Owen had full-on dreds way down past his shoulders then, which Mum hated and Louis found amusing, but Herod's hair was just a stringy, greasy mess. He was wearing an unwashed grey t-shirt and jeans: weird because before Herod always used to smell of Pears soap, cinnamon, mixed with the underlying wet-earth scent of china clay. I could see the confusion in Mum's eyes: it was as if Herod were turning into someone else, a strange and terrible butterfly hatching from a chrysalis. He was also extremely thin. We were always kind of lanky, my brothers and I, but Herod's wrists looked as if they might snap.

"Darling," Mum said, too brightly. "We saved you some supper."

And the empty expression spread across Herod's face again: he simply disappeared while you were speaking to him, leaving only the shell of his body behind.

But this was the first time the Creature spoke through him.

"Mother," he said, as if speaking to a small, stupid child, "you must think I'm a fool. I know what you put in my food. I'm not going to fall for it. I know you're poisoning me, you bitch."

Herod would never have called Mum "Mother", or "you bitch". Or said "fool" like that. You could tell it wasn't really him speaking, that he'd become a kind of mouthpiece for something else. It was just that we didn't know what.

After he'd gone, letting the door slam shut behind him, Mum was the first to speak. "He needs to see someone, Louis. Quickly." She turned to me. "Herod's not very well, Jack. He didn't mean what he said just then. He really didn't."

The next day when Yvonne dropped me home from school, Louis was there but Mum wasn't.

"It's Herod," Louis told me. "He's gone into hospital. He's going to be OK, though. They just need to keep an eye on him for a while."

"Why?" I demanded. "What's wrong with him?"

Louis didn't answer for a moment then said, "Well, I suppose it's like this: he's confused about what's real and what's not."

The difference between fear and reality is a fine line and Herod had crossed it. Imagine not trusting the people you love, afraid they're trying to kill you. If it sounds scary that's because it is.

Herod didn't come out of hospital for weeks and by then I hardly recognized him. The drugs make you fat – even

Herod, who was always so skinny. The next time he went to hospital, though, he stayed for longer. Much longer.

"You saved my life," Herod told me when he was in hospital that second time. "You're a fucking jailer – you know that, don't you? I'm a prisoner and I was nearly free, but you had to stop me."

I turned and ran out of the room, stood in the hospital corridor staring blankly at a poster about hand hygiene. A nurse rushed past. Mum followed me out – I knew she would.

"Jack," she said, hugging me. I could smell her spicy perfume mixed with the cucumber scent of hand cream. "You did the right thing. You did."

I wasn't always so sure.

The last time I'd seen Herod was just before Christmas, months ago now. He walked down the sweeping gravel drive to meet us, early on a frost-bitten morning. Had he been listening for a car? The Peace Centre is a stately home that got taken over by a load of Buddhists in the seventies, an old house with pillars outside the front door and a thousand glittering windows, hidden from the world by parkland dotted with trees, a half-frozen lake. The roof was still white with frost when we arrived.

Herod still looked like Owen, of course: dark, catlike, but thinner and quieter. He shaved his head now but wore the usual ragged jumpers, workboots, old jeans. He smiled when Mum handed him a big squashy Christmas present wrapped in paper decorated with silver reindeers. They hugged, then Louis stepped forward. I hung back.

"I know you said you'd rather I made a donation to charity," Mum said, speaking a bit too quickly, defensive, "and I did. It's just I saw this in town and I thought about you."

I knew what it was: a jumper, really soft wool. Expensive. I'd seen it on the kitchen table that morning. She was doing what she could for him: there was no proper central heating in the Centre and, despite the wood-burners and fireplaces, it was always freezing.

Herod smiled his quiet smile again. "Thanks, Mum."

"Hi there!"

I glanced across the courtyard. A tall woman with bushy brown hair emerged from the barn, carrying a basket of logs. She waved eagerly, striding over to join us.

"Morning, Andy," Herod said. He smiled at her, gently, as if she was somehow fragile and might shatter into pieces like a dropped glass. Andrea never looked fragile to me – she must have been nearly six feet tall, dressed in dodgy ethnic hemp clothes that billowed in all the wrong places. Always hanging around, somehow.

Mum and Louis smiled at her, too.

"Come and join us for a cup of tea," Herod said. He didn't really have much choice – Andrea was still lingering with the basket of logs, obviously waiting to be asked.

She gave him the thumbs-up sign and disappeared into the house through a side door.

"Poor girl," Mum said. "She always seems a bit lonely."

There was the usual small, awkward pause before Herod turned to me. "How's it going, Jack?"

"Fine," I said. "Fine."

I flicked my unfinished cigarette out of the bedroom window. Mum or Louis had put some music on downstairs – Joan Baez. It's what Mum always listens to when she's in a state.

And now Herod was gone. Just gone.

EIGHT

Enough of the charming memories, I told myself. The house fell quiet as the last track finished on the CD. Most Sunday nights we got a film out, so Mum and Louis were probably watching one downstairs, but I was pissed off with them for being so weak, for going along with Bethany's bitch of a mother, and they'd come rushing back from France straight into a shit-storm of my creation. It wasn't exactly a cosy situation.

So I went out. I took the unconventional route through my window, dropping down onto the corrugated-iron roof of next door's potting shed. No point in bothering Mum and Louis again. They had enough to worry about and, anyway, they thought I was getting an early night. I didn't really know where I was going, only that home was stifling me and I had to get away.

I crossed the park and sat on a bench near the pavilion, staring at the tall, narrow old houses fronting the green. The lights were lit up at ours. It looked friendly, welcoming – a place you'd want to be. Well, I didn't. Not tonight. I still had a tiny bit of sticky left, so I got out my smoking tin (it had once contained those weird boiled car-sweets). I skinned up, wondering what I was going to do.

Bethany and I had made a silent pact to see each other. Putting it into operation was going to be tricky. We weren't at the same school. If I called her house and someone other than Bethany answered, what would I do? Hang up?

Maybe she could call me. Mands and some of the other girls from school had rung me the odd time, like when Jo Brinkley and me were in that sappy play together. Or when I got put with Georgie Hicks for the Geography project.

I shivered, thinking of Georgie. She's not bad, quite pretty really. But I couldn't forget the way she'd stared at me across the table, stupid triangular graphs spread out between us.

"If you ever want to talk about anything, Jack, you know I'm always here, don't you?"

I didn't answer. Jono once said to me, "Listen mate, given the state of you it's a good thing your family's even weirder and more fucked up than everyone else's – the girls can't get enough of it. They all want to help you get over your inner demons. You're sorted."

Personally, I found that a little creepy.

But Georgie Hicks hadn't called for a while. I'd made

my feelings pretty clear. Either way, Mum and Louis were bound to get suspicious if they answered the phone to a girl asking for me. It was clear they both thought Bethany's mother was poisonous, but they'd basically agreed with her. If they found out we were seeing each other, life would soon become very unpleasant.

I sighed, blowing out a cloud of smoke. I'd have to use Sammy as a go-between. Bethany's mate from the girls' school wasn't to be trusted – she'd obviously blabbed to someone about the festival.

They could pass on messages; Jono at a push. Bethany and I would meet in secret. Maybe after a while her mum would chill out and come round, and we wouldn't have to be so ridiculously 007 about all this. It had been pretty obvious that the idea of splitting us up came more from her mum than her dad.

I knew what I needed to do. I had to see her. Now. I had to tell her my plan.

Bethany lived in one of the big houses right on the outskirts of town – twenty minutes' walk down past the church. But I bumped into Jono – literally – while I was still in the park. We crashed into each other just past the big old wrought-iron lamp post in the middle of the green, neither of us properly looking where we were going.

"Shit!" I said, before I realized who it was. "Sorry."

Jono barely seemed to notice that we'd smashed right into

each other. He grabbed me by the arm. "Jack," he hissed. "I was just going home to call you –" it was a good thing he hadn't: Mum thought I'd gone to bed early, but she might still have come upstairs to see if I was awake enough to speak to Jono – "I was down at the Spar and I saw Ben Curtis."

I stared at him a minute, getting my head around the fact that Jono and I were now running on different tracks. He'd just got home from a festival: he was knackered. He'd be going to bed soon, ready to wake up for school. I'd entered another world, one where Bethany's parents had forbidden us from seeing one another, and Herod was missing, being searched for by the police.

"So what?" I asked. Ben Curtis is this career dope smoker in our year – bit of a knob, really. Kind of guy who gets all snitty if you skin up and there's a wrinkle in the spliff. Uses a rolling mat, takes it all far too seriously.

"He had a broken nose, Jack."

"And?" I shrugged, impatient. I wanted Bethany. Nothing was going to stop me getting to her: not her mother and definitely not Jono in a stress about Ben Curtis's nose. He's well ugly, anyway: a broken nose would most likely be an improvement.

Jono sighed, looking at me as if I was a complete idiot. "Buggy did it. Ben owed him nine quid."

I stared at him, fully concentrating now. "What? *Nine pounds*. Are you serious?"

There were implications. Buggy and I had an agreement.

It was a small town. I'd been buying dope off him for over a year now. He'd given me the lovely sticky on credit. A whole quarter. I owed him twenty quid. It was cool, I'd thought at the time, because I was waiting for my Christmas cash from Dad (six months late, but never mind). I'd rather eat my own face than ask my father for money, but I wasn't about to turn down a Christmas present. I'd have it any day now, swore to Buggy he'd get what I owed him by the end of the month.

"You didn't pay him," Jono asked, "did you?"

Well, there was no use in Jono panicking all over town. I smiled, patting him on the arm. "Look, mate, don't worry. It'll be fine. Buggy and me had an agreement. He was happy to wait till my dad's cash turns up. It should be in my account by the end of the month. I'll pay Buggy then. It's cool. For all we know, Curtis has probably been bullshitting him for ages about that money. It's not the same situation at all."

Jono frowned, nodding. "Maybe. Ben's definitely a massive bullshitter. But still. You don't want to mess with Buggy."

"Don't worry," I said again. "I can handle him. And anyway I've got more important stuff to think about – me and Bethany got caught. Mands' cousin blabbed about her coming to the festival with us – you know, Bethany's mate."

I kept quiet about Herod and about Owen. If I'd seen Sammy, I would have told him. Just not Jono. What was the point? I've known Jono even longer than Sammy and he's good for a laugh; its just everything is always about him.

"Shit!" he said, and then straight away: "My mum reckons I stayed at yours all weekend—"

I sighed. "Don't worry. She's not going to see my parents, is she?" And I told him what had happened when I got home.

Jono winced. "Nasty, mate, nasty." I could tell he was mostly relieved that his mum was blissfully ignorant about the whole thing. Jono's mum is blissfully ignorant about most of what Jono gets up to, to be honest.

"We don't care, though," I told him. "I'm going to see her now."

Jono stared at me. "You must be well desperate." He sighed, properly patronizing. "Why bother with the hassle? Georgie Hicks blatantly fancies you – and she's easy." He shook his head, looking annoyed. "They all think you're so bloody mysterious. I don't get it. You're just a dodgy greb with long hair."

He didn't understand about Bethany – that was for sure. "Thanks for the compliment, Jono." I crossed the park at a run.

I'd never been to Bethany's house before but I knew which one it was. One of the very last places before town gave way to fields. Almost in the countryside, really. No wonder she rode a bike. She'd told me her bedroom looked out over a meadow, which meant it must be round the back.

There was a big ornate gate at the top of the driveway, but it was open, hanging rusty off its hinges. That surprised me. Bethany's mother seemed like the type who'd go in for closed gates everything all neat and tidy. Her dad was off sick in a new job, though. What happened if you couldn't go to work for months because you were ill? Perhaps Bethany's parents weren't as loaded as they seemed. I avoided the gravel drive and made for the back of the house, sneaking round the side of the garage.The garden was enormous – mainly lawn, stretching away into nowhere. A few windows were lit up, but all had the curtains drawn save one on the first floor. I heard the muffled hum of a television. Sitting room. I grinned to myself, sticking two fingers up at the curtained window.

There's one for you fascists.

From the middle of the lawn, I looked up at the lit window on the first floor. A string of fairy lights blinked behind the glass. It was Bethany's room. Had to be.

For a minute I stood there like a complete idiot, wondering what to do. Then I remembered something I'd read in a Famous Five book when I was a kid, took a small stone from the gravel path running round the back of the house and lobbed it up at the window. Not a bad shot, from someone as rubbish at sport as I am. It bounced off the glass and landed on the grass beside me. I waited, breathless, half expecting someone to open the sitting-room curtains and peer outside. Nothing happened. Then, slowly, the upstairs window opened and Bethany looked out. She saw me and smiled. Holding a finger to her lips, she disappeared for a moment. I waited, feeling like my hair was turning white with fear.

And yet, strangely, getting a kick out of it, too. Nothing ever happens around here. This was something.

After a while, a small pale thing fell out of the window and floated to the ground like the petal of a rose. I ran forwards and scrabbled around in the damp grass.

Bethany had thrown me a note, a message. I read it, blue Biro on graph paper: BACK DOOR OPEN.

Grinning, I felt my heartbeat speed up as I pocketed the note. I wasn't about to leave the evidence lying around.

I'd passed the back door already. Avoiding the gravel path again, I retraced my steps. I had to take a couple of deep breaths as I reached for the handle. If I got caught, that would be it. Mum would take me to the cleaners. She doesn't get properly angry very often, but when she does, it's awful. I shuddered, but I couldn't help feeling pleased with myself. I listened outside the door but all I could hear was the sound of the telly, still muffled.

There was only one solution: not getting caught.

I opened the door and went in, finding myself in a hall. To my left, there was a rack of neatly ordered shoes and boots, including Bethany's wellingtons. To my right, coats on hooks. I could tell where the sound of the television was coming from now: behind a closed door a few feet down the hall. There were the stairs, rising up in front of me like an invitation. I know where the creaks are at home, but this was like playing Russian roulette backwards. Each bullet chamber in the gun holding a bullet one. The chances weren't good.

I made it up the stairs, breathing easier now. I could hide more easily up here if someone heard me, opened the living-room door downstairs to check it out. The upstairs corridor was dimly lit: pale, creamy walls and pictures of flowers. It was more like a hotel than a house. At home, there are embarrassing photos of everyone splashed all over the walls, faded posters from exhibitions Mum's been to in glass clip frames, a charcoal sketch I'd made of our old cat, Loopy, on the kitchen wall. When Loopy died, Mum got it framed. There was nothing like that in Bethany's house. It was sterile.

A door at the far end of the corridor had been left ajar, casting a thin line of flickery light out into the corridor. Bethany.

I went in, closing the door behind me. Bethany was sitting cross-legged on the bed, waiting, still wearing her pink dress, but now her legs were bare, which for some reason gave me more of a kick than if I'd found her wearing nothing.

She watched me, her face serious, black hair loose and winding around her shoulders, almost down to her waist. I hadn't realised how long it was. "I knew you'd come."

The room was a complete contrast to the rest of the house: a cave of fairy lights and colour. Old metal signs advertising chocolate and cigarettes, photos tacked to the walls, Indian scarves trailing everywhere. A garland of fake roses. Her bed was an old iron one, like something out of the Victorian times, the sheets white and crisp.

Saying nothing in reply, I walked till I was standing just inches from where Bethany was sitting. I can still remember the heat spreading through me, a kind of wild crazy excitement I'd never felt before. She stood up and we kissed, hands in each other's hair. It was hard to stop, but Bethany pulled away.

"What are we doing?" she whispered. "Oh, God, what are we doing? They're downstairs—" She broke off and looked away for a moment, taking a long breath. "Sit down," she said, and I did. We lay next to each other on the big white bed, holding hands, legs twined together. "I'm sorry," she whispered, holding my gaze. "About my mum – what she said. It was awful. I thought your mum was going to cry."

"It's OK," I said. "It's OK."

Mum had cried but I wasn't going to tell Bethany that, make her feel even worse. She already had to live with the woman.

"You don't have to tell me if you don't want to," she said, "but what really happened to your brother? Herod, I mean. I don't believe what Mum told me – I know she got it from that stupid friend of hers."

Well, I knew that already but I could never bring myself to tell Bethany I'd overheard that conversation.

So I told Bethany about Herod. "They both got really into free parties," I began. "Well, Owen did and Herod followed him. It was a big deal at the time, wasn't it? Raves. The thing was, Owen could take ten pills on a Friday, smoke a quarter, sleep it off and be fresh as a daisy the day after. He'd do it again on Saturday night and play Scrabble with me on

Sunday evening looking as if he'd spent the weekend hiking in the countryside."

If I closed my eyes, I could still see him, sprawled out in front of the sitting-room fire, swigging from a glass of Louis' finest red.

"Qi," Owen said. "It means 'force of life'. Thirty-three points, Jack. You've got to learn all these two-letter words, man. They'll win you the game."

Bethany waited for me to go on, stroking the back of my hand with one finger.

"Herod," I said, "was different. They're identical twins but he wasn't the same kind of person at all. Herod's kind of fragile. Gentle. Owen was really clever at school, but Herod could only do Art. He was brilliant at it, though. He used to make these sculptures out of porcelain that looked like leaves. He thought about stuff too much. Smoked too much weed.

"They were doing their A Levels, going out a lot. Herod had this job in a health food shop, saving up for Art Foundation, but he got fired. So whenever there was a party going on or whatever, Owen paid for him – he worked in a café down by the station. It's closed now. We had an agreement never to ask our dad for money. Then … you know sometimes people go on about getting the fear when they've had too much to smoke?"

Bethany nodded. "Yes, like Jono did in the field. I never have. Maybe I haven't smoked enough."

"I've never had it either, but Herod did. And it got worse

than that. He wasn't just a bit paranoid. We didn't know till later, but he'd started hearing voices, bad voices telling him horrible things. Eventually, Mum realized there was something really weird going on and sent him to a psychiatrist. He was taken into hospital, stayed for ages. Then a few months later, he had to go back for even longer." I sighed.

"Was everything all right?" Bethany said, quietly. "What happened in the end?"

"So, basically, Herod got sectioned again. Fully sent off to the loony bin. He'd taken too many drugs and went psycho, just like they tell you in the *Daily Mail*. He was literally psychotic: hearing voices the whole time. Everyone blamed Owen for getting him started in the first place, or Owen felt like they did, so he went off travelling and never came back for uni. And that was it. Haven't seen Owen since – till the weekend."

"Where's Herod now?" Bethany asked.

Good question.

I suppressed a shudder. "While he was still sectioned, he had to stay in hospital. That was pretty dark. But then once his medication got sorted my dad paid for him to go to somewhere better – this properly expensive place full of ageing rockers with coke problems. Anyway, Herod got into Buddhism, so now he lives at a retreat. Gets up before dawn to meditate, does advanced yoga, all that stuff. They say it helps keep the mind on track. I don't know whether that's true or not but he's off medication now. You can tell:

he's lost all the weight. It'd made him really fat. He doesn't even drink now, or hardly at all anyway. Just the odd beer." I tried to sound casual, but in the back of my mind all I could see was Herod's face, how firmly he'd held that last white plastic tub of paracetamol. He'd meant to die: they found a note afterwards. I never knew, though what it said. Everyone always says that suicide is gutless but it also takes a kind of courage. "But now he's left the Peace Centre," I said, finally. "We've just found out. It's why Mum and Louis were back early. No one knows where he is. My mum even called the police."

"No way," Bethany whispered. She looked up at me. "That's awful. You poor thing, Jack."

I wanted to stay lying by her side all night, just us.

I hadn't even come here to tell Bethany about Herod, so what was it about her that had made me spill my guts?

"I reckon I know what we can do," I said, thinking it was time to change the subject.

There was no discussion, no sidestepping. No playing hard to get. We were staying together and I don't think either of us questioned it for a second.

I told her about Jono and Sammy. "They'll be our go-betweens," I said. "They'll definitely do it. We can arrange to meet through them, but I don't reckon we should call each other. It's too risky."

Bethany stared at me, deadly serious. "I shouldn't be doing this at all. I know I shouldn't."

For one awful, belly-churning moment I thought she was going to do the sensible thing and finish with me. Instead she let out a long breath, pushed back her hair and reached out, taking my hand, gripping my fingers hard with hers.

"I shouldn't be doing this," she repeated, in a whisper, "but I'm going to do it anyway. I want to see you. This weekend. I've made plans."

A quick hot flame of excitement flared in my stomach. "And what," I said, "are those plans, exactly?"

Bethany turned and kissed me again, pulling away before I had the chance for more, gave me a dangerous smile. "Mr and Mrs Ferguson," she said, "are old family friends. She was at school with my mum – they're the only people my parents really know around here, and they're having a big party this Saturday night. They live in Hamble St Margaret. You can get the bus there. Bring Sammy and Jono, too – if you come around nine o'clock no one's going to notice. John Ferguson's a champagne dealer, so they'll all be really pissed. And by the way, it's fancy dress."

I smiled, holding on to both of her hands. She knew I'd be there, but now it was time to go.

Leaving her that night was one of the hardest things I've ever done.

NINE

I had another nasty surprise just before last lesson on Monday afternoon. As Sammy and I were leaving Maths and heading to Art.

"I can't believe you did that," Sammy was saying. "What if you'd got caught in their house? Jesus Christ."

I grinned, patting him on the shoulder. "But we didn't, did we? So are you coming to this party on Saturday, or what?"

Sammy sighed. "All right. Sounds a bit scary, but if there's free drink and sexy posh girls, I'm in. So did you do anything then? With Bethany?"

At least Sammy doesn't think he's the world's expert on women like Jono. I shrugged. "Nothing I haven't done before." Somehow, I didn't want to talk about Bethany that way. She wasn't like other girls – not that I'd got particularly far with any of them, either. Unlike Jono, who"d lost his virginity in a car park in the Christmas holidays with Georgie Hicks's older sister. He made up for the complete lack of style by shagging a girl in the year above us, which I have to admit is pretty impressive. Elle Hicks isn't bad, either, although why she'd gone for Jono, God only knows.

I looked up. There was someone standing in my way, blocking the double doors out of the Maths block. It was Ben Curtis. His nose really was a mess, swollen and ugly. The bruising had spread to his eyes, blackening both of them like he was some kind of nightmare panda.

"Bloody hell," muttered Sammy.

"All right, Ben?" I asked, calmly. He'd owed Buggy nine quid. I owed Buggy twenty. OK, so both amounts were peanuts, but still, Buggy obviously didn't think so.

"What do you think, Jack? Do I look all right?" I struggled not to laugh when Ben spoke. He sounded like Donald Duck. "Buggy reckons you're next," he said. "He's after you."

"OK, no worries." I wondered why the hell Buggy had gone back on our agreement. "I'll just find him tonight." The end of the month, I'd promised him. He'd agreed. But then Buggy wasn't the kind of guy you messed with: if Buggy changed his mind, he changed his mind.

Ben gave me a sarcastic look. "Right," he said. "You go looking for him. Right. Just watch out, Jack. How do you reckon I explained this to my mum? She thinks I fell down the stairs."

He shoved past me and was gone, and it was a good thing he didn't see me trying not to laugh. But really. You had to see the funny side. It was like a rubbish, small-town version of *The Godfather*.

All the same, I didn't have a clue how I was going to get the money. I couldn't ask Mum or Louis. Mum was suspicious enough already – if I started asking either of them for cash she'd be convinced I had a massive smack habit or something. There was no telling her I could smoke a few joints and be fine.

"Christ," Sammy said again. "What are you going to do? I'm skint or I'd borrow you some."

"It's fine," I told him, breezily. "I'll sort it out."

In the end, I did something desperate. Something stupid, in fact. Something I'd always sworn not to do in a situation like this. I called my dad. Using the payphone in the hall outside the secretary's office, I tried the San Francisco number. I've got a direct line, but was only seven in the morning there and I wasn't sure anyone would pick up. In the end, it rang through to a receptionist rather than his PA.

"I'm sorry, sir, can I ask who's calling?" The receptionist sounded suspicious, wondering how I'd got hold of the private number.

"It's Jack," I said. "His son," I added, after another icy silence.

"Oh…" There was a pause. I imagined her checking a list of approved callers. "Well, honey, I apologize, Mr

MacNamara is at a conference in Tokyo this week. It's kind of late out there now, but I can place a call to his personal assistant for you." Now she just sounded sorry for me.

Don't worry, love, I thought, *I'm used to it*.

In one second flat, I was transferred. "This is the office of Edward MacNamara." A smooth, young-sounding voice. A man this time.

"Can I speak to him, please? It's Jack."

This time there was no pause. The guy was obviously better trained than the first flunky I'd spoken to. He knew exactly who I was. "Jack! Hi. Your dad will be so pleased you called. He's with a client right now but I can have him call you once they're done at the restaurant. Is there any message?"

I was starting to feel like a real idiot now, but I was desperate, OK? There was no point in asking Dad to phone me back. He hardly ever did. There was always a good reason, but all the same, he wouldn't call. Or not till it was way too late, anyway. "My mum said he'd given me some money for Christmas and, er, I haven't had it yet. So I was just wondering where it was. I've been saving up for a new bike."

It's so easy to lie over the phone.

"Oh." There was a slight pause. Maybe the guy was embarrassed at Dad's laxness. It was June, after all. "Well, Jack, I'll chase that right up for you."

"Thanks." I put the phone down, shaking my head. I don't let that stuff get to me. It's just the way it is.

The PA was probably the one who'd reminded Dad to

give me a Christmas present in the first place. I bet he's got a list: that old aunt of his, Blanche, in San Francisco, Owen, Herod, some secretaries and clients. And me. Oh, and the girlfriends – however many he had at the moment. One had been enough to push Mum over the edge, but I knew that he sometimes operated more. I thought of the blonde woman in the lobby of that London hotel, years ago – her high heels and polished fingernails. Had Dad had ever seen her again?

"I'll transfer a couple of hundred. Sterling, not dollars." I could imagine Dad barely looking up from his desk. "See to it, will you?" The bank forms were probably still sitting in his in-tray, waiting for a signature.

It must have been a continual mystery to my father how he ended up with kids like us – a super successful software genius with a couple of waster crusties and a layabout teenager for children. He probably blames Mum. My parents started off in the same place, but they've ended up being polar opposites of each other.

I remembered how Mum once slammed the phone down, hanging up on him.

"What now?" Louis had said.

"He's suggested boarding school for Jack," Mum spat. "So typical. He completely ignores the boys for years and now he can't, he thinks it's time to throw some money at the problem."

"Boarding school?" Louis repeated.

"No way," Mum said. "No way. It's another world, all that money. We'd never get Jack back. We'd lose him completely."

So Dad just kind of got further and further away till he wasn't even really my dad any more.

He kept that promise he'd made to me in London, though. Not long before Herod went into hospital the first time, I flew out to San Francisco with the twins.

We walked out into the arrivals lounge, Owen rolling up a fag the second we got out of baggage reclaim, ready for lighting outside. Herod was very quiet with that blank expression again. It meant he was hearing voices, but I didn't realize that at the time.

I thought Dad would be waiting on the other side of the barrier. "Wow," I'd imagined him saying, "Jack you've grown so much I hardly recognize you." Well, I'd hoped that was what he'd say.

But Dad wasn't there. A jumble of unfamiliar faces, people shrieking out names, running towards each other, hugging, laughing.

"Fuck's sake, not again," Owen muttered, dropping his rollie back into his smoking tin. He patted me on the head. "Come on, J. We'll find a cab. H, where are you going, man?"

Herod turned to look at us, shrugging. "I'm going to look at the arrivals board. I think we might have come in a bit early. Maybe we should wait."

"I wouldn't bother," Owen replied.

"Look," I said. "Over there." In amongst the crowd waiting for our flight there was a grey-haired, Spanish-looking guy, holding up a placard with MACNAMARA printed on it.

Owen laughed. "It looks like we'll be in time for our conference after all, boys."

He started walking towards the guy with the placard, hefting his rucksack over one shoulder.

Dad was always at work by the time I woke. Herod and Owen used to sleep till almost lunchtime while I wandered around the house, barefoot on polished wooden floors, looking at the weird pictures on the walls, watching MTV and the best cartoons I'd ever seen on a telly with a massive screen – it seemed like there were ads every five seconds. Sometimes I swam in the square blue pool. One day, when I was exploring, I discovered a room at the top of the house. There was an artists' easel, a trestle table covered in tubes of paint, a mug with a smear of black coffee in the bottom and a green glass beer bottle. Canvases leaned up against one wall, splashed with bright paint. So Dad was an artist, too – like Herod. Mum hardly ever talked about him and I realized there was a lot I didn't know. I looked at the paintings for a long time, trying to find some clues about my dad. All I could see were puddles of colour.

On our last day I woke up much earlier than usual. I could smell coffee brewing; I knew he was still there. I went into the kitchen. As usual, breakfast was already laid out on the table – there was a Puerto Rican woman called Rita (pronounced "Heater") who came in every day and was well suspicious. She kind of hovered, like she was hoping to catch one of us going through Dad's pockets or something. Anyway, Dad was standing by the window. The house was on a hill; there was an amazing view of the city below and, in the distance, a strip of electric-blue ocean.

"Hello." Dad turned around, smiling at me. It was six thirty in the morning. "Want some coffee?"

I liked the way Dad always spoke to me as if I was another adult. He passed me a cup without waiting for an answer. Silently, I went and stood next to him at the window. He looked down at me. Smiled. I took a swig of coffee, hot and bitter.

"You're really getting kind of tall." He shook his head, staring out across the city again. "Time passes, I guess."

"The paintings upstairs – what are they of? All those colours," I said, and suddenly got really embarrassed. I'd basically just admitted to sneaking around the house.

Dad didn't seem to mind. "Music," he told me. "I like painting music. I'm synaesthetic – it means I see music and numbers in a different way to most people. Every note has a colour, so does each number."

I stared at him. "What happens when you do long division or something? What happens to the numbers?"

Dad smiled. "They change colour. If I close my eyes, I can see them doing it. Do you want to come into the office with me today?"

"OK," I said, dizzy with joy.

What I remember most about the office was that no one wore a suit and tie – one guy was wandering around in Bermuda shorts with no shoes on. There were even people playing table tennis. I sat on the sofa in Dad's office and drew, using up sheet after sheet of paper, wishing I could see music. He wasn't even there most of the time but I was happy.

All through Art, I sat doing nothing, gazing out of the window. I couldn't help wondering what it would take to bring Dad home. Make him step back into our lives like a character in a play. Act Four. *Herod*, I found myself thinking. *Would he come back for Herod?*

"Jack? Where's your still-life orange?" I looked up. Mr Trelawney was standing by my table. The others sniggered – Georgie Hicks who'd been freaking me out by staring at me all lesson when she thought I wasn't looking, Joe Simmonds, Naomi Briggs – all of them except Sammy. Trelawney's all right. Younger than the other teachers by about four hundred years, but still pretty ancient. Maybe mid-thirties or something. He's our form tutor as well. We were lucky.

When I first had Trelawney for Art last year, he said to me, "I remember your brother, Herod. A very fine ceramicist. How is he getting on these days?"

Most people are afraid to mention Herod's name, but not Mr Trelawney. And he didn't remember the Creature; he remembered Herod – the fact that he was really good at ceramics. I liked that.

I'd got in at half twelve the night before (through my bedroom window – I wasn't taking any chances), collapsed into bed and rushed out of the house this morning at quarter to nine with a bit of toast in one hand and my bag in the other. "Sorry," I told Trelawney, "I forgot to bring my sketchpad and stuff. Can I give it to you tomorrow?"

Mr Trelawney gave me a look. "The same tale you told Mrs Wright about your Maths? Ten minutes late for registration. Not a great day for you so far, is it? Wait behind after the lesson, Jack. And get on with some work, for Christ's sake." He didn't seem annoyed with me, though. Something else. Worried.

Probably remembering Herod, I thought. *Wondering when I'm going to go off the deep end.*

Just after we got back from San Francisco, about a week before Herod went to hospital the first time, Mr Trelawney brought him home one night. Mum, Louis and I were watching some crap on TV about detectives. It was quite late but nobody had told me to go to bed. Mum and Louis had other stuff on their minds. Owen and Herod were out; we thought they were together. It was dark and the curtains were drawn. The window had been left open slightly, though, letting in the warm smell of Mum's lavender plants. Mum flinched when a car pulled up outside. It was almost as if she knew. Straight away, we heard voices in the street.

"The thing is, you don't understand: they won't let me

work. I can't get any peace. I can't, oh, God—" Herod was speaking quickly, each word strangled as if his throat was rigid with fear.

"Herod, you can't stay in the Art Room. You need to be at home, mate. It's late. It's Friday night."

Mum rushed out of the room and Louis turned to me and said, "Jack, maybe it's time you went to bed."

I didn't; I followed him into the hallway where Mum was answering the door to a man I'd never seen before and Herod, who was hollow-faced, eyes darting everywhere, his clothes covered in clay – even his hair was grey-streaked. The man was Trelawney – younger then, early twenties. Dressed in jeans and a hooded top, he didn't seem like a teacher. Just worried.

"Mrs Lefebvre?" he asked. "I'm sorry to intrude—"

"Just let me stay, take me back," Herod snapped. "I don't need to be here. It's pointless."

"Herod," Mum said. "Come in, darling. You look tired." She glanced at Trelawney. "Thank you so much. I don't understand. Where was he? Herod, where have you been?"

"I left my wallet in the classroom," Trelawney said. "Herod was there when I went back for it. Some amazing work he'd done. Really beautiful. Your son is very talented." He shook his head. "But the school won't allow it – students on the premises after hours. It's to do with insurance. I'm sorry."

Herod pushed past us all, including me, and ran upstairs. Unseen, a door slammed.

Trelawney shrugged, looking helpless – embarrassed, even. "I don't know, Mrs Lefebvre, if you want to look into it, but there's a few places in town renting studio space to artists."

"That's a good idea," Louis said. "A studio of his own. He's got so much creativity he doesn't know what to do with it, that boy."

"Yes," said Mum, "perhaps that's it. And thank you again, Mr Trelawney. Have a good weekend."

Was Trelawney remembering that night, too? Waiting for me to go off like an unexploded bomb from the Second World War. I had a distant hope he might forget about keeping me back after the lesson, but no such luck. No one had the decency to distract him; there was no acting up, not even from the usual suspects like Ginge Philips. So when everyone was bundling out of the classroom for break, Trelawney caught my eye.

"Don't think you've slipped my mind," he said. "Wait." I stopped, and he shut the door. "Normally, Jack, I like the cut of your jib. Keeping your head down, quietly getting on with your own thing. You're clever – you know how to keep people like me off your back. So why did you come in this morning completely unprepared for a school day?" His tone of voice changed very slightly. "Is there something wrong?"

"No," I said to Trelawney. "Nothing's wrong." I couldn't help glancing down at his desk. One of the drawers was open and I could just see a leather wallet shoved in among a jumble of paper clips and manky old pastels. A crisp purple twenty quid note was poking out. There for the taking. I wondered how easy it would be to come back in and help myself. Just as a loan. I'd return it, obviously, at the end of the month.

"Jack?" Mr Trelawney was staring at me now. I couldn't blame him; I was acting pretty weirdly. "Are you sure there's nothing I can help you with?"

"Sorry," I said, looking him in the eye. "It's just that I slept really badly last night, and then I forgot to pack loads of stuff this morning."

"Insomnia? Does it happen often, Jack? You should get it sorted out – you can see a doctor about that kind of thing, you know."

"No," I said. "It's not that bad. I'm fine. It was just a one-off."

Trelawney frowned slightly. "All right, then. Try reiki. My girlfriend swears by it. And if there's anything you want to get off your chest, Jack, I'm here."

Trelawney let me go, but I knew he'd be watching me.

TEN

There was this really lame science club after school on Monday. You had to go to it if you were doing separate Biology at GCSE. It sucked, but I wasn't about to annoy Mum even more by not going, and Trelawney obviously had his eye on me. It wasn't till then that I had my idea.

Mrs Hannay had us watching this really boring film about how they make baked beans (yes, really). It was hot in the classroom and a lone fly circled above the TV. Everyone was yawning, even Mrs Hannay, who must have watched that film, like, a hundred times.

The TV was a brand-new one.

"Thank goodness," Mrs Hannay had said, rolling her eyes. We'd spent all of last term whacking the old one every five minutes till the wavy blue lines disappeared from the screen.

I bet Bethany didn't have to put up with this at St Agnes's. I thought of her, still beautiful even in the disgusting burgundy St Agnes's skirt, hair very black against a white shirt. It seemed so ludicrous, somehow, that we were on opposite sides of town, trapped in different schools. I glanced around the shabby classroom. I'd grown out of this place. I should have been somewhere else, with Bethany. On an empty beach in the rain, in the middle of London, even, anywhere except this shit-heap of a town. Just me and her.

And then Buggy crept into my daydream and that was it.

Maybe, I thought, *maybe if I can't pay Buggy in actual cash, I can pay him with something else. Something he can sell on if he wants to.*

It was a shame. I liked Mrs Hannay: she was all right, even if she did have a moustache. I was still going to steal her TV and sell it to my dealer, though. Even then I knew it was ridiculous. Where did I think I was living? South Central LA?

I did it anyway.

"You're a nutter," Jono hissed at me as we crouched beneath a window of the science block, Sammy was beside us. It was pretty creepy being in school at night. The playground was dark and empty. A lone crisp packet skittered across the concrete. The windows glittered. It was eleven thirty, it would be Tuesday morning in half an hour, and it was cold.

I glared at Jono, but Sammy spoke up first. "Are you sure you want to do this? Can't you just borrow the cash from

Bethany? She goes to a posh school – she must be loaded—"

"Don't be a wanker," Jono interrupted. "Obviously he can't ask his girlfriend for money. It's not right, is it?" He stared at me, shaking his head. "I don't get why you never ask your dad. He's minted. My mum says he's got millions. Millions! It's crazy. I mean, for Christ's sake, how cool is that?"

Jono's dad was a personal trainer. He lived in Cyprus with a second wife who only looked about five minutes older than Jono. Jono's dad was too busy shagging to do much else.

I shrugged. What was there to say? Jono was right: I should have been blagging cash off my dad every five minutes. He's got enough and he must feel guilty – we never see him. But there was the pact. The promise I'd made with Herod and Owen. I wasn't about to explain that to Jono.

Sammy sighed. "All right, all right. How do we get in? Slaphead must've locked up."

Slaphead was the caretaker – a skinny old weirdo with a big shiny bald patch. His house was right next to the school. He'd definitely call the cops if he saw us, just for being on school property after hours.

I got up and walked to the door, feeling in my pocket. There it was, my bus pass.

"What the hell are you doing with that?" Jono demanded, under his breath.

"Watch and learn," I replied, and slid the bus pass into the crack between the door and the frame, holding down the handle. I'd read about this trick but never tried it. To be honest, I didn't really expect it to work. Surely Slaphead would have bolted most of the doors from the inside?

"I think," Jono whispered in a voice dripping with sarcasm, "that you're meant to use a credit card."

"I haven't got a credit card, dickhead."

I was more surprised than Sammy and Jono when the lock clicked and the door swung open. For what felt like hours we stood there staring at the dark, empty corridor. Then suddenly we all moved at once and rushed in, Sammy closing the door carefully behind us. Inside, the stench of cheap bleach and detergent burnt my nostrils. Without saying a word, we headed to Mrs Hannay's classroom. Our boots squeaked on the polished floor: Doc Martens are a nightmare for breaking and entering. I was first to reach the door. It was unlocked.

I wondered how Herod had felt that night he broke into the Art Block, the night Mr Trelawney found him. If I could bend time, shape it the way I wanted, I might run down the corridor, run through five years as if they were doors opening one after another and find Herod there in the Art room, pouring life into a hump of dead clay, alone with just one light flickering overhead.

"The security here's crap," Jono whispered. "They're asking for it."

We went in. There was a lingering smell of fags. Old Hannay must've sneaked a crafty smoke after school, doing her marking. Who could blame her? Considering none of us had ever burgled anything in our lives before, we operated like a well-oiled machine. Jono knelt down to unplug the shiny new TV. Sammy and I took an end each.

"You owe me for this," Jono snarled.

"Yeah, yeah. When was the last time *you* bought any weed?"

"Oh, piss off."

"Come on!" Sammy looked terrified. "Let's go."

"Not yet," I said. "Insurance."

"What are you talking about?" Jono hissed.

"Look, either wait here or follow us." I led Sammy off down the corridor towards the art room, the pair of us hugging Mrs Hannay's TV. Jono followed. I knew he would.

I don't know why I did it. I just couldn't stop myself. We put down the TV outside Trelawney's room and I reached out for the doorknob. It was like looking down at someone else's hand. *I'm not the kind of person who does this,* I thought. *This isn't really me.*

I wasn't really expecting the door to open. Trelawney was probably supposed to have locked it, but I knew he didn't always remember.

"What is he playing at?" I heard Jono say.

"Mate—" Sammy sounded worried. Well, he had good reason to be. The longer we stayed, the likelier it was we'd get caught. And we really, really didn't want to get caught.

I walked over to Trelawney's desk, the drawer still jammed open by the jumble of sketch books, receipts and other crap inside. I actually couldn't believe my luck when I saw it.

Mr Trelawney had forgotten to take his wallet out of the desk. I reached out, opened it.

"You idiot," Jono whispered. "Sam, stop him."

"What are you doing?" Sammy demanded. "This is too full-on. Nicking the TV was funny. This is just dark. Put it back."

"Pack it in, Jack!" Jono sounded really scared.

"Just in case." I folded up the twenty pound note and stuck it in my back pocket. "Better to be safe than sorry."

"You've lost the plot," Jono muttered, and Sammy just said, "Let's get out of here."

I wasn't going to argue with that.

So we ran, Sammy and me doing this weird crablike sideways dash across the playground with the telly, which was getting heavier by the second, followed by Jono. We made it to the fence, Jono got over. We passed him the TV and then legged it off down the riverbank back towards town taking turns to carry the TV. When we got to the green, we finally stopped running and slumped onto a bench, breathless and weeping with silent laughter. The further away from school we'd got, the funnier it'd seemed. It was a relief to sit down. I put the TV on my lap, leaning forwards to rest my head on top as I caught my breath.

"What are you going to do with it now?" Sammy asked, rubbing his arms. "That thing's heavy. I mean, you can't exactly take it home, can you?"

Jono yawned. "I don't know about you, but I'm going home. I'm knackered. You so owe us, Jack."

"Fine, fine," I told him, "like I said, next time, you buy the draw, Jono. I'm taking this to Buggy's."

"What, *now*?" Sammy asked.

"The chippy's open till one, isn't it? He'll be there. Look, don't worry about it. You both go home, get some sleep. I'll deal with this. It'll be fine."

"What if he turns nasty?" Sammy demanded, shivering and rubbing his arms. It was getting even colder. There were no clouds in the sky.

"How can he? It's a brand-new telly, virtually. Worth at least forty quid and I only owe him twenty. Once this is delivered, Buggy's going to owe *me*."

They both just stood there staring at me like I'd lost my mind, so in the end I just picked up the telly and walked away.

Home, sweet home. I went in round the back again, onto the roof of next door's shed, muscles in my arms shrieking as I pulled myself up and through my bedroom window. Buggy had taken the TV, all right, and then demanded the cash as well. Great, just great. I could have nicked the twenty quid and saved myself the hassle.

At least Buggy was dealt with, though. Problem solved – or at least I thought so.

I left the window open just a crack and crouched on the floor a moment, catching my breath. I could hear voices, people talking – not just Mum and Louis, by the sound of it. They were in the kitchen, two floors below, so I couldn't make out who was speaking. It was half twelve at night. Who would come round at that time of— Then it dawned on me. Owen had come back at last. He really had. I sat on the bed, kicking off my boots.

Everything was changing; it was doing my head in. Would he still be here in the morning?

I thought of Bethany, asleep in her white bed on the other side of town, trapped in a house ruled by a witch. I would have given anything to be away with her, somewhere far off, just us together. None of this. Four days. Four days until I could see her again.

I opened my bedroom door and stepped out onto the landing.

Very clearly, I heard Mum laughing. Oh, yes, Owen was definitely back.

I went downstairs, opened the kitchen door, blinded at first by the bright lights. Louis was leaning against the Aga, opening a bottle of champagne. It was quarter to one in the morning. Owen and Mum were sitting at the kitchen table with a girl I'd never seen before. She was pale and leggy, with long red hair.

"Jack," said Louis, "just in time to get some glasses."

Mum frowned at me, her smile disappearing a moment. "I thought you'd gone to bed?"

If only you knew, dear.

I was still *persona non grata* and Owen could tip up like the prodigal son and get toasted with champagne.

"Homework," I said, automatically reaching into the cupboard for glasses. The red-headed girl was looking at me. Why were they all so bloody cheerful and smiling? Herod was missing and they were knocking back the bubbly stuff. It's the kind of effect Owen has on people. But when I handed Mum her glass, I could see in her face that she was wearing the *It's OK* mask. I wondered what she was thinking about behind the mask.

"Jack," said Owen, raising one eyebrow at me. No one would have guessed that a few days ago we were at a festival together: he had the sense not to mention it. "This is Natasha," he went on, resting a hand on her shoulder. "We're having a baby."

Speechless, I looked at her again. The redhead was skinny, leggy, draped in glittery Indian scarf type things. I suppose she might have been pregnant somewhere under there.

Only Owen could turn up out of nowhere with a girl nobody had met, announce that he'd knocked her up and get a reception like this.

"Nice to meet you, Jack," Natasha said, smiling. I couldn't help but admire her cool.

"Yeah," I said. "You, too." I took a swig of champagne. It wasn't as if I had much choice.

ELEVEN

It was Friday lunchtime. Jono, Sammy and me were having a crafty fag on the back field. The teachers can never be bothered on Fridays, so I knew we wouldn't get caught.

I lay on my back with one hand resting on my shirt pocket. I could feel Bethany's folded letter inside. Bethany had given it to Amelia, who'd given it to Amanda Blake and Amanda had given it to me, saying breathlessly, "It's so romantic, Jack. I mean, Bethany's so gorgeous and her parents must be really strict. It's like a fairy story."

More like a total hassle than a fairy tale. It hurt, not being with Bethany – I felt a dull ache the entire time, like hunger. *Why can't I just be with her?* I asked myself a hundred times a day, cursing Bethany's mother every way I knew how.

Bethany had written on an ordinary sheet of A4 graph

paper, using thick black fountain-pen ink. I'd traced my eyes over every smooth, sloping letter. I liked her handwriting – it wasn't round and babyish like most girls' with stupid circles or hearts over the "i"s.

"What does it say, then, this love letter?" Jono asked, sarcastically. "What does she want?" Then he said something really gross. I probably would have found it funny if he hadn't been talking about Bethany.

"As if I'd tell you, anyway," I replied. "Look, she just wanted to make sure we were still coming to the party on Saturday." That wasn't all the letter said, obviously.

Dear Jack, I've got to see you. I'm counting the hours till the weekend. Are you still coming? If you reply to this, I wish I could keep your letter. But I won't be able to – I'll have to burn it. I don't trust Mum not to search through my stuff. I hate her. I can't wait to see you.

I wouldn't write; I'd already decided. The words never come out how I mean them. I'd phone her, hang up if her parents answered. I knew her number by heart, even though I'd never actually called her house.

"What do you reckon?" I said. "Are you guys coming or not?"

I tried to sound offhand but actually the thought of gate-crashing some really posh party without Sammy and Jono as accomplices was kind of scary. It's one of those things that's funny if you do it with friends, terrifying on your own.

"May as well," said Sammy. "Why not?"

Jono just shrugged but I could tell he was up for it.

"We can't just turn up with nothing, then," I said. "Bad form. It's a party."

Sammy rolled over onto his back, puffing smoke up at the grey sky as he lay next to me. "What, are you talking about scoring? Sounds like more trouble. Anyway, aren't we all skint? There's going to be loads of free drink – may as well just stick to that."

"Don't be a gay," Jono replied. He really is a brainless caveman sometimes. Usually. "What about your sister? I bet she could sort us out."

Sammy shut his eyes, half dozing. "No good. Leila's doing another festival for Mum and Dad – some boring poetry thing in the middle of nowhere. Left on Wednesday night."

I stared up at the clouds. "Well," I said, "Owen's back, isn't he?"

Jono and Sammy both rolled over and stared at me, grinning.

"Why didn't I think of that?" Jono asked.

"Because you're an idiot," I told him, sighing. "Don't worry. I'll sort it out."

Sammy gave me a look, clearly thinking about the Buggy/Mrs Hannay's TV situation and not wanting to repeat it any time soon. "Are you sure that's a good idea?"

You had to admire him for speaking his mind, even when it made him look like he was just scared of getting caught. The way I saw it, if we were going to get spotted by Bethany's parents at this jolly old party, I'd far rather be off my face when it happened.

I called Bethany on Friday night. Mum and Louis were in the kitchen, making supper and drinking wine. I stood by the desk in Louis' study for what felt like years before I finally picked up the phone.

My heart was banging like crazy. *Calm down*. I thought. *Calm down. If someone else answers just hang up*.

The phone rang four, five times before someone picked up.

"Hello?" It was Bethany. Relief washed over me like someone had just poured a bucket of warm water down my back.

"It's me."

"Oh, yes, that's OK. See you on Monday." Bethany wasn't making any sense, but even just hearing her voice was enough to make me want to run across town; I would have given anything to be with her. I realized one of her parents must be standing near by, listening in.

"We're coming tonight. We'll be there." I took a long breath, not wanting to sound like an idiot. "Listen, I can't wait to see you. I miss you."

"Me, too," she said, softly, and then, "Yeah, I'll bring the notes from yesterday. OK, bye."

Bethany hung up, and I stood there with the phone in one hand, stupidly not wanting to let go of it. It was my last link with her. I looked at my watch. It was nine p.m. *Twenty-four hours*, I told myself. *Twenty-four hours till we're together.*

I counted every one.

Jono and I were crammed into the back of Yvonne's car, next to a load of empty plastic crates. I couldn't stop yawning – I was knackered. I'd slept badly; every time I closed my eyes Bethany was there, yet not there. It was torture.

Sammy was in the front, fielding enquiries from his mum.

"I know where the commune is. It's on the road outside Lower Wenlock." Yvonne sounded harassed. "What I want to know is why you're going and why on earth you're so desperate to get there right this minute." We'd caught Yvonne on the hop, just as she was getting ready to leave for a meeting with some woman about chutney. She stopped at the lights, drumming her fingers on the steering wheel. We were heading out of town. We'd already passed Bethany's house. I'd forced myself not to stare as we went by, wondering what she was doing. It was early, not even half nine. Was she thinking about the party? Was she thinking about me?

"It's my brother," I said. "Owen. He's staying there for a bit."

Yvonne turned and stared at me. "*Owen?* Really?" I could tell straight away she was wondering why Mum wasn't giving me a lift out to see my long-lost brother if I was so desperate for his company.

The lie slipped off my tongue like warm honey. "I wouldn't have asked, only Mum and Louis are busy this morning, and I just really wanted to—"

"Oh, please," Yvonne said, quickly. "I've just realized the less I know about this, the better." She sighed, and switched on Radio 4.

Beside me, Jono smirked.

We pulled up on a tiny lane, just by a fence made of woven willow branches. "The commune's in there," Yvonne said. "You'll have to walk a fair way down the path, but you'll find it. I'll be an hour with Jeanette, and I've got stuff to do back in town, so don't be late. I'll see you here at quarter to twelve. OK?"

We bundled out of the car and she drove off, leaving us in a cloud of exhaust. For a minute we stood in the lane like a bunch of idiots, ducking into the hedge when a Land Rover shot past.

"How does your mum know about this place, anyway?" Jono asked. He looked slightly nervous and I hoped I didn't. I couldn't help feeling a bit nervy, launching myself into the midst of a load of random crusties.

Sammy shrugged. "Some bird that works for her and Dad used to live here. Come on. She meant it about not being late."

I found a gap in the hedge and, silently, we trudged down a path shaded by trees. We were in a wood. It was kind of pretty, with stripes of golden sunlight pouring down between the trees, puddling all over last autumn's dried leaves. I could smell smoke from a fire, but there was no other sign of life. "Are you sure this is the right place?" Jono muttered, kicking aside an overgrown tangle of bracken. "It's the middle of bloody nowhere. Why didn't Owen and his woman stay at yours?"

I shrugged. "It's where he told Mum they'd be. Till next week – then they're off to see Natasha's parents in Scotland. You know what he's like."

After a bit, the smell of woodsmoke got stronger and the path opened out into a clearing. I don't know what I'd been expecting but it wasn't much of a commune: a couple of vans, a knackered old London bus with ivy growing up the wheels and one massive tipi. Someone had drawn birds on the tipi canvas in faded fluorescent paint, but that must have been years ago. The remains of a campfire smouldered next to a crumpled beer can. A tin mug lay on the ground. On the far side of the clearing, I could just see an old guy with grey dreds chopping logs on a tree trunk, but he didn't notice us.

One of the vans was Owen's Sprinter. Or perhaps it was Natasha's.

I realized that Jono and Sammy were both staring at me, waiting.

"Well," I said, "that's Owen's van. I reckon we'll go and wake him up."

I knocked on the side of the van and for a minute nothing happened. Then the double doors at the back opened. Jono and Sammy shrank away, leaving me standing there alone.

It was Natasha, wearing an old white shirt and not much

else. Red hair everywhere. She smiled, managing not to look surprised.

"Jack," she said, as if we'd just met in the street. "How are you?" In the morning light, I could see a spatter of gold freckles across her nose and cheekbones. I was trying not to look at her long, pale legs. I could see past her into the van – a double mattress on a plywood platform behind the front seats, a small bench with ethnic-looking cushions crammed in opposite a wood-burner.

"Fine." I really didn't know what else to say.

Natasha smiled again. "Owen's asleep. Listen, I'll wake him up. Why don't you get the fire going?" She handed me a fire-blackened steel kettle and a jerrycan that sloshed when I took it. "There's a pile of kindling behind the van. Should be some newspaper under the tarpaulin. You've got a lighter, haven't you?"

Laden with hippy camping gear, I wandered over to the fire, dazed, Jono and Sammy scurrying after me.

"What did she say?" Sammy hissed as we squatted by the fire, blowing frantically at the tiny, flickering flames I'd managed to stir up. "Is that really Owen's girlfriend? She looks like a model."

"Ginger, though. Shame," said Jono, with an annoying air of long experience. "Bet she's got a firecrotch."

"Shut up!" hissed Sammy. "Bloody hell!"

I looked over my shoulder and there were Owen and Natasha, ambling over to the campfire. He had one arm slung around her shoulder, carrying a handful of mugs. She was holding a carton of UHT milk and, thank Christ, was now wearing a long silky skirt and flip-flops. I didn't think Sammy would have been able to cope with her legs otherwise; I knew I couldn't have.

Owen smiled at Sammy and Jono. "Hello." It was hard to tell if he recognized them or not; either way, he made it seem like he did.

"I'll leave you to it, O," Natasha said. Then, turning to Sammy and Jono. "Would you two like to come and have a look around?"

I thought Sammy was going to faint. Jono just about managed to smile and mutter, "Yeah, go on then."

And I was alone with Owen. At first he said nothing, just chucked a load more kindling onto the pathetic fire I'd made. The flames leapt into life and I felt like an idiot.

"Put the kettle on, then." Owen squinted across the clearing, raising one hand at the old guy chopping wood, who returned the greeting. "My head's killing me. Nige brews his own cider and it's murder."

Fumbling, I poured water into the kettle and sat it in the fire, just near the edge.

"Well, what can I do for you?" Owen said.

Now it was just the two of us, I couldn't bring myself to speak. I just looked at the kettle, steam rising from the spout.

"Quiet, aren't you?" Owen watched me, obviously amused. I noticed he still wore an earring: a tiny silver loop halfway up the lobe. "So he's gone, then." Owen rolled a fag and held the tip to a flame, taking a deep draw. He was talking about Herod. I hadn't expected that. "They told me last night but I had this feeling there was something up with him before we got back. Couldn't get it out of my head. We were in France." He blew out a cloud of smoke. "We were coming home anyway – felt like doing Glastonbury this year. Drove all night from the South to Calais. Fucking silly, really. I still don't know where he is."

"The kettle's boiling."

Owen reached for a stick, hooked the kettle out of the fire and, wrapping the sleeve of his jumper round the handle, poured boiling water into two mugs. The teabags floated to the surface in a swirl of milk. Everything he did was confident, precise. "Hope you don't take sugar. We haven't got any."

"It's OK." It wasn't what I'd come to ask but I said it anyway: "Where do you think he's gone? They've called the police." Only this morning, I'd overheard Mum and Louis talking quietly in the kitchen, thinking I was still asleep.

"What worries me is that he's ill again, badly, in hospital somewhere," Mum had said. "What if he's been sectioned with no ID on him? They won't know who he is."

"Ed made you think that," Louis told her. And the police have checked all the local hospitals, haven't they? For all we know, Herod's gone on holiday. Maybe he just didn't bother telling Andrea. Last time we were there he was fine. Totally fine. Didn't you think so?"

Mum had sighed. "Well, yes, I did. I just wish he'd phone. Sergeant Prentice said there'd been no sign of him at all yet. Nothing. Maybe we should go down there, Louis."

Owen fished the teabag out of his mug and threw it into the fire, taking a long swig. He shrugged. "I don't know where Herod is. I just don't know." He turned, watching me with those tilted, golden-yellow eyes. "Why did you come, anyway?" He smiled, faintly. "You didn't bring your mates out here to catch up with your dear old brother, did you?"

Suddenly, I felt ashamed: it was pretty shallow, the reason why I'd gone. It wasn't as if I owed him anything, though. Owen hadn't sent me so much as a postcard in five years. I drank some of my own tea, biding my time before answering, but I couldn't shake off the impression that he knew what I was doing, was secretly laughing at my tactics. "We're going to a party tonight."

It was all I needed to say.

Owen laughed. "For Christ's sake. Come back after five years and everyone still thinks I'm a drug dealer. Whoever it is you're trying to impress, she's not worth it."

He didn't know Bethany. He didn't know anything about her. He'd touched a nerve, though. Why was I really doing this? To impress her? *Do you honestly reckon she's going to think you're cool for scoring a load of nasty speed?*

I would be with her again in a matter of hours; that was all I cared about. I ignored the small, quiet voice whispering, *Is this party thing a good idea?* Mum would never let me go if she knew about it. She was in enough of a state about Herod. *But she's never going to find out, is she?*

I was on edge waiting to see Bethany again.

"What do you know about it?" I snapped at Owen, furious with myself for letting him get to me. I glanced away, took a steadying breath. "Have you got anything or not?"

Owen watched me over his mug. "You make me feel old." He looked up at the sun slanting through the trees. He'd never worn a watch. "Early still. Your mates wouldn't be too happy being dragged all the way out here for nothing, would they?" He sighed, chucking the dregs of his tea into the fire, getting to his feet. "So are you coming or not?"

I could see Yvonne's car waiting in the lane as we trudged back down the path. She'd kept the engine idling.

"What did he give you?" Jono had demanded, as soon as we'd left the tipi behind.

"I don't care," Sammy said. "It was worth it just to see your brother's girlfriend. She's—"

"Five months pregnant," I interrupted. Jono and I laughed. I patted Sammy on the shoulder. "Don't worry about it." I reached into my pocket and produced a jiffy bag bulging with a tangled brown mess of stalks, unable to stop myself grinning. "Approximately one thousand magic mushrooms."

"Oh, my God," Sammy said, and Jono just laughed. I'd done it, or rather Owen had.

"Now all we've got to do," I said, "is find some fancy dress."

That took the smile right off Jono's face.

TWELVE

Luckily, Mum didn't notice the bottle of Strongbow half hidden by Jono's bag when she came into my room that evening.

"OK, we're going." She sighed, leaning in the doorway. "I'd rather not, but anyway. If anyone rings, you will take a message, won't you? Call me at the college if there's a problem. Number's in the book."

"I'll be all right," I said.

Mum gave me a steely look. "I hope you're going to prove that I can trust you again, Jack. I can, can't I?"

"We're just hanging out," I replied, feeling properly guilty.

You see, if my parents were really strict, I wouldn't mind lying to them. But even Mum and Louis wouldn't have let me go to meet Bethany at a party I wasn't invited to.

"Good." Mum frowned. "I've just got a bad feeling about tonight, that's all. Maybe—"

But then Louis called for her up the stairs. It was time to go.

"Have a great time, Caroline." Jono treated Mum to one of his cheesiest smiles and to my disgust she smiled back. Jono's full of himself as it is.

And that was it, job done. When the sound of our ancient Ford coughing into life in the street below had faded, it was time to deal with the fancy dress issue. I'd found a Sainsbury's bag full of horrible old clothes in the bottom of Mum and Louis' wardrobe, including several really rough silky shirts right out of the eighties, with baggy sleeves and frills everywhere. They were kind of piratical.

"Bloody hell," Jono kept muttering as he buttoned his up, "I can't believe I've got to wear this. It smells of B.O."

"It doesn't," Sammy told him. "That's just you, mate."

We looked ridiculous. Sammy was wearing a wig with an attached pirate's hat; Jono was sporting a pink Afro – I don't know what that had to do with anything, but he seemed happy with it. I'd put my hair in a ponytail (rank) and tied a red scarf of Mum's around my head. I looked like a massive loser, and it was only going to get worse later when I added the beaded mask Mum wore to a belly-dancing hen-night for one of her awful friends last year. The thought of Mum belly-dancing still makes me shudder.

All the same, better to wear a mask and look like even

more of an idiot than be recognized by Bethany's parents.

"I can't believe we're doing this," Jono said as I locked the back door behind us.

"Well, how else do you suggest we get there?" I went over to the lean-to and pulled out Louis' bike, followed by my old one from when I was, like, twelve years old. "Walk?"

I looked at the shed, the window overgrown with ivy now. Herod wouldn't be able to see out if he still worked in there.

"It's only five miles," Sammy said, breezily. "It'll be fine, Jon. Come on. It's going to be so worth it when we get there."

"Fine." Jono shouldered his rucksack and reached for Louis' bike. "You two gay boys can share, then."

"No way." I handed him my old mountain bike. "I'll give Sammy a backy, but we definitely get the biggest bike."

It was quarter to ten by the time we finally arrived in Hamble St Margaret, absolutely knackered. I really don't recommend giving anyone a backy for a five-mile bike ride. The three of us had to take it in turns in the end and walked the last mile.

It must have been loads worse for Sammy and Jono: all I had to do was think of Bethany, closer and closer to me with every second.

"I'm ruined," Jono moaned, flopping down on a grass verge by a phone box, letting my old bike clatter to the ground. We collapsed beside him. "That's just taken, like, ten years off my life."

"We've run out of cider, too." Sammy lay on his back,

sweat pouring down his face. Not a pretty sight, but then I wasn't looking my most attractive, either. Great. Just great.

"Still got the shrooms, though." I stuck a hand into the pocket of my rucksack, making sure. "Let's have some now and save the rest."

Another thing I really don't recommend is eating a load of magic mushrooms without anything to drink. I thought I was going to throw up: it was like chewing a mouthful of stringy soil.

Luckily, it wasn't hard to find the party, once Jono and Sammy had stopped pissing themselves with laughter at my belly-dancing mask. Hamble St Margaret is basically just a few houses, even smaller than that tiny place we'd caught the train to the weekend before. The enormous white marquee in the garden pretty much gave it away, along with the strains of a band playing bad funk.

"Music sounds rubbish," Jono said, frowning.

I was still half gagging on the soily taste of the mushrooms and was in no mood for whinging. "That's not what we're here for, is it? Think of the birds, Jonathan, think of the birds. All those lovely girls in there just waiting for a man like you."

"Are you taking the piss?"

"Come on, you guys, shut up," Sammy said. "We've got to look confident. As if we belong, not bickering like a pair of old women."

Sammy's not usually your man for confrontation or taking the lead; Jono and I were so surprised we just got up and followed him. We stashed the bikes in a hedge along with our bags and, calm as you like, strolled across the back lawn of an old place with pillars by the front door. You could see straight through the huge windows to the other side of the house; it must have had enormous rooms. We never made it inside, though. The action was all in the garden but so far all the party promised was a bunch of wrinklies dressed up as vampires and cowboys, and a couple of harassed-looking waitresses in black and white. The waitresses gave me the fear: what if someone from school was working here tonight? A couple of the girls do waitressing and they're the idiot type who definitely can't keep their mouths shut. They'd blow our cover, but there was no time to worry about that. It was time to get in there.

Bethany would be wondering where I was.

"Oh God," muttered Sammy. "What are we going to do?"

The marquee was seething with people in fancy dress, and whichever old trout had thrown this party had clearly invited quite a few people our age, so we didn't look that out of place. It was lucky we hadn't arrived any earlier. Empty coffee cups and plates smeared in chocolate, cream and fag ash were still scattered across the tables: they'd only just finished dinner, and waitresses were moving the last of the tables away from the dance floor. The funk band was playing, but hardly anyone was dancing. A couple of pissed women older than Mum lurched around just in front of the stage. I would absolutely die if I saw my mum doing that. They were twirling each other about and laughing. Just at the side of the stage, a guy of about eighteen with a smooth, tanned face was chatting up a younger girl: she was super skinny with Bambi eyes and a silky dress that none of the girls in my year would have been able to afford in a million years.

We were way out of our depth. I scanned the marquee but couldn't see Bethany anywhere. The air was thick with cigarette smoke and boozy breath. Empty bottles of champagne littered every available surface: the waitresses couldn't get to them fast enough.

"Bloody hell," Jono hissed into my ear. "There's a line of coke on that table." I glanced over my shoulder. He was right. What kind of party was this?

"Look," Sammy whispered again. "She's coming over."

An older waitress with a black skirt pulled tight over a fat belly was making her way towards us, professional smile fixed on her face. She was holding a tray of glasses.

Was she going to ask us to leave? I looked around for Bethany again but instead I spotted her mother, whippet-thin, wrapped in a gold lamé dress. She was wearing a black, fringed wig and an enormous necklace: Cleopatra? I thought my heart was literally just going to stop. The sound of the party faded: the funk band, the loud babble of drunken chat, the clinking of glasses all drained away. Facing us now and smiling, Angela knelt down to talk to a couple of little girls dressed as witches. It was the first time I'd seen her smile properly, nothing fake, and it made her look like Bethany.

I stared, terrified but unable to look away as the kids each grabbed one of Angela's hands, dragging her right past us onto the dance floor. It was probably one of the most frightening moments of my entire life. Her eyes were ringed with heavy black make-up and they travelled over the three of us without a flicker of recognition. Then she was gone, dancing with the little witch kids right in front of the band.

At that moment, the waitress reached us. "Drink, sir?" she said to Jono.

I felt so weak with relief I wanted to sit on the floor.

"Why, thank you," said Jono in a fake posh accent, and took a glass of champagne, followed by Sammy.

"Sir?" said the waitress to me, and I picked up the last drink on the tray, resisting the urge to hold the cold glass against my forehead. I took a swig: my second dose of champagne in a week. Wow, I was really moving up in the world. It made a change from Strongbow.

A second later, the waitress was gone, and I turned to the others. "You're on your own. I've got to find Bethany."

Jono rolled his eyes and Sammy started rolling a fag. He was scared, not wanting to show it. "Don't know what's going to happen when we start coming up on the shrooms," he muttered, draining his glass. "This is weird enough as it is."

Jono and I started giggling like a pair of girls. I mean, it was pretty ridiculous. "I've said it before and I'll say it again," Jono told me. "You must be well badly desperate, Jack, getting us into this."

I saluted them and launched myself into the party. I finished my champagne and casually grabbed another glass from the tray of a passing waitress: now she did look familiar. Wasn't she in the sixth form? I didn't care.

I was there for one reason only.

THIRTEEN

I walked through the marquee, trying to look as if I belonged there – confident and slightly bored, fast getting extremely drunk. Bethany wasn't with any of the girls I passed. They were glossy-haired, in costumes obviously geared up to making them look hot: a belly dancer (pass), a slightly over-weight fairy (fail). There was a lot of feathery, floaty stuff going on that I couldn't make any sense of at all, and one girl dressed as a nurse.

When I found Bethany, she was sitting around a table towards the back of the marquee with a vampire and an old bag dressed as a judge. Bethany wore a white lab coat. A pair of goggles rested on her head. The lab coat was open. Underneath it she was wearing a cotton dress and a silvery cardigan. She wasn't taking any of this seriously. She was streets ahead of every other girl in that tent.

The old bag had style: I mean, she was necking back the bubbly stuff and must have been ninety, at least. Her judge's wig was slightly drooping forwards over one eye. Bethany laughed at something the old dear said: a real laugh, tipping back her head, right from the belly. The middle-aged vampire did a kind of sneer and lit a cigarette, making a big deal out of topping up everyone's glasses.

Bethany took her refilled glass and, over the rim, she looked straight at me.

I looked at her.

Everyone else in the tent seemed to disappear. It was just us.

I walked towards her, and it sounds nuts, but I felt as if I was flying, my feet not touching the ground.

I stood by the table, heart pounding. "Hi."

"You seem to have an admirer, Bethany," said the vampire, sarcastically.

"Good thing, too," the old lady said. "Top me up properly, Robert, if you can bear it. There's no need to be stingy."

Bethany ignored them both, getting to her feet. She smiled at me and laughed again. She wasn't wearing much make-up – a bit of silver glitter on her face. She made every single other female at the party look like a gargoyle in lipstick. We stood facing each other, holding hands, her fingers warm. It was so hard not to kiss her there and then.

"We can't walk out of here together," Bethany said, quietly.

"It's too dangerous. See you outside."

I smiled at her, turned and walked out of the tent, into the garden, where shadows were gathering and the day's warmth was just starting to ease off.

I walked right down the lawn and waited for her by an apple tree.

I watched her following me; I loved to watch the way she walked. Slow and relaxed, like she had all the time in the world.

When Bethany reached me, we held on tight, hands in each other's hair. *At last, at last,* I thought, feeling relieved. When I kissed her, I tasted cigarettes and champagne. The same warm, lemony smell rose from her skin.

"You did it," she whispered, smiling up at me. "You did it."

"Did you think I wouldn't come? You'd have been talking to a judge all night."

"I knew you would." She laughed. "I hope I'm as mad and drunk as that when I'm old. Let's get out of here. There's woods backing on to the garden."

"No way," I said. "You're not getting away that easily." I bowed at her. "Shall we dance?" The branches on the apple tree were swaying, but there was no wind. Owen's little present was starting to kick in.

"It's stupid because this was my idea, but I'm really scared of being seen." Bethany smiled again, looking nervous.

"Why do you think I brought a mask? It's so rammed on the dance floor no one's going to notice. It's like some kind of mosh pit full of old people."

Bethany laughed. "All right, then. I can't resist a pirate. That *is* what you're meant to be, isn't it? I'm a mad professor."

"Wait." I reached into my pocket. I wanted to take her with me. "Give me your hand. Would you care for a mushroom?"

"A what?" Then Bethany laughed, and swallowed a handful, washed down with the last of her champagne. That's the way to do it.

After that, it was all a bit Thank-you and goodnight, ladies and gentlemen. We swept back across the lawn, hand in hand; I felt like I could breathe again properly now she was here, as if all week a great heavy weight had been pressing against my chest.

Now it was just me and Bethany.

Everyone and everything else was nothing but a blur of colour and light. We went back into the tent, danced, holding each other, lost in the gathering crowd. The champagne lake had done its work and now pretty much everyone was dancing, or trying to: a sweaty tangle of glitter, fur, sweat-shiny skin and swirling black cloaks clouded by cigarette smoke.

Time flashed by; I don't think we were at all scared of being caught any more. We just had each other, circling slowly around the dance floor, close together. I was still wearing my mask. I saw Sammy once, talking to an old guy in a cowboy hat, and Jono twice. He was with a different girl each time.

I saw Bethany's dad, too, sitting at a table towards the back of the tent: tall and very thin, dressed as a knight, talking to an overweight woman in medieval gear who smiled too much.

At last, Bethany drew me away from the crowd. The funk band had long since packed up; a floppy-haired blonde guy was DJ-ing (badly) – playing a load of seventies stuff like Abba and the Stones. I didn't mind the Stones but Abba was too much.

We went outside into the cool night, back among the apple trees. Bethany was breathless with laughter, lab coat drawn tight around her shoulders. I was freezing but I wrapped her in my cloak (an old dining-room curtain: properly sad but neither of us were complaining).

"You must be freezing." She held me closer and we pressed against each other, leaning back on the apple tree. I could still hear the music: it was getting worse and worse, but somehow it was funny.

"Not with you here," I said, and she handed me a cigarette.

What she said next totally threw me.

"Jack, are you OK?"

I blew out a cloud of smoke, feeling cold inside, like something bad was going to happen. "Why wouldn't I be? I'm here with you." I smiled.

Bethany shrugged, looking suddenly awkward and quite sober, as if she'd remembered we'd only met each other a few weeks before. There was so much about each other we didn't know. I dug the fingers of my free hand down into the grass, holding on to the world as it was.

"Well," she said. "Your brother – Herod. I mean him being missing and everything. I've been thinking about it all week. I feel so bad about my mum, what she said. She can be such a stupid cow."

I could have cried with relief. Honestly. I thought she was about to end it. There'd been a shadow in her eyes when she spoke.

I told her about Owen and Natasha, how they'd come home.

"It's because they're twins," I said. "Owen and Herod. They're kind of weirdly connected. Owen said he just had a feeling that he had to come back."

"No sign of Herod, then?" Bethany went on, taking the cigarette, eyes fixed on me. The silver glitter had spread all over her face now. She shone, full of light, but that was really just the mushrooms. "Isn't that a bit weird? I mean, wouldn't he phone?"

"The police are looking for him." Saying so made it more real. I shut my eyes.

"Oh, Jack," Bethany whispered. She reached out, pushed the hair away from my eyes. Her touch was hot; it burnt me.

"She called my dad, too. Not that it'll make any difference. I don't know why she even bothered. He doesn't give a toss about us."

"I'm sure he does," she said. "You're his kids."

"I haven't seen him for two years. He lives in California."

Bethany frowned. "That's really shit – even if they are divorced and everything. It doesn't sound like he makes much of an effort."

"He doesn't. He's a twat, anyway. I don't care."

Bethany turned to face me, serious. "Oh, come on. You don't need to lie to me. I can tell that you don't really think that."

"OK, I do care. It annoys me that he doesn't bother. It's just so lame. I'm used to it, though."

What I liked was the way Bethany didn't try to tell me everything was going to be all right. Her total honesty.

I took a long breath. She waited for me to speak. Was I really going to say it, after all these years? Admit it to someone? Those counsellors had tried everything short of the rack to get this out of me. Was I now going to unload it onto a girl I wanted to be with every minute of the day, a girl with long dark hair and silver light around her face. I could almost hear Jono's voice in my head: *Shut up, Jack. Do you want her to think you're a pussy?*

The words spilled from my lips anyway.

I closed my eyes. I could see it all.

"Tell me," Bethany whispered. "If you want to."

Once I'd started talking, it was hard to stop. "OK. You know how I said Herod went to see a psychiatrist. They sent him to hospital and he was there for weeks whilst they tried to get his medication sorted out."

Bethany just held on to my hand, waited. This was the first time it had ever felt right to talk about what had happened to Herod.

"When Herod came out of hospital the first time, it was like he'd been changed into someone else," I said. "I was only about ten – it was pretty freaky. You know how I said the antipsychotic drugs made him fat? Well, it wasn't just a bit. He got really massive. He'd stopped saying weird things, though. He used to get this blank look on his face before – when he was hearing voices – and that totally stopped as well. And he wasn't interested in clay any more, either. That really was strange."

"So was Herod a proper artist, then?" Bethany asked.

I nodded. "He made these amazing sculptures of flowers and leaves, that kind of thing. The school used to order in porcelain clay just for him. All his work was paper-thin – really delicate. But the medication he had to take stopped all that. Herod said it shut down his mind; he hated that even more than being fat. He said it was like being in a house with most of the rooms locked. He'd missed too much school to go back, but he volunteered with a conservation charity for a while, although that stopped after a bit. He wasn't OK. Not really. We just wanted to think that he was."

I stopped. The whole thing replayed in my head like a film. It was the school holidays. Summer. Mum was at work and it was only ten in the morning, so Owen was out somewhere, still in the middle of the night before; I was at home with Louis and Herod.

"This bloody student, Jack," Louis told me, "has written a thesis so completely boring that I am falling asleep. I need coffee. Will you be OK for fifteen minutes while I run to the shop?"

Both of us thought Herod was just hanging out in his room as usual. He couldn't sleep at night so he used to stay in bed most of the day.

"I'll be fine," I said, "as long as you get me some crisps."

Louis laughed. "Maybe – if you're lucky." I was never one of those kids who wished their parents would get back together: Louis was a hell of a lot nicer than my dad. Even I could see that. Louis always had time for me.

I still don't know what made me go upstairs. It was very quiet, but the radio was on downstairs in the kitchen. The sun was shining on the stairs, showing up the dust in the carpet.

"One day," I told Bethany, "I went up to Herod's room. He was sitting on the bed, facing the door, holding a white bottle of pills. Paracetamol. 'I just want it to be over,' he said. There were two more bottles lying on the floor with the lids off, empty. He'd taken the lot. You don't even need that many."

Bethany sat silently, waiting for me to go on. Saying nothing, she stroked the back of my hand with one finger. I was starting to feel cold, sitting out there by that apple tree, but her touch sent waves of heat rolling through me.

What are you doing? I asked myself, furiously. *We're at a party. We're meant to be having a good time*. I was going to bring her down, massively, but somehow I just had to say it.

"I kind of ran at him and knocked the last bottle out of his hand. He was chewing like crazy and there were pills all falling out his mouth. He was trying to wash them down with wine. He had this bottle open.

"I managed to get to the window. I yelled for help and Louis was down there, my step-dad, just coming back from the shops. He called an ambulance and they pumped Herod's stomach at the hospital."

That wasn't all they'd done.

I remember the frozen fear on Louis' face as he looked up and saw me, dropping his bag on the pavement as he ran to the front door. The plastic bag split and a silver pack of coffee skidded across the concrete.

"He tried to kill himself. That's mainly why Herod was sectioned that second time – you know, forced to stay in hospital. That time it wasn't just a few weeks. They gave him loads of drugs. He was there for ages."

I stopped talking and lit a fag, taking a long, deep draw. Bethany put her arm around my shoulder. We leaned together. I felt relieved, lighter somehow, as if I'd finally just put down a heavy load. "What a horrible, horrible thing to see," she said, "your own brother in a state like that, wanting to die."

I could tell her anything. I trusted her.

I stared at the cigarette smoke, feeling dizzy. The champagne bottle was cold in my hand. I took a swig but I could barely taste the stuff any more, just sugary sweetness on my lips.

"So," I said, just to break the silence, really, "I can see why your mum freaked out when she found out who I was. My brother smoked too much dope and went mad, tried to top himself. At least now you know what really happened." I paused. "Look. I'll understand if you don't want to know. I mean, I'm a fuck-up."

Bethany frowned. "Give me the champagne." She took a swig and turned to me. "I think I'm falling in love with you, Jack."

I stared at her; I forgot everything else.

I answered with a kiss. Five minutes later, it all began to fall apart.

FOURTEEN

"Bethany!" I heard someone say. "I've been looking for you everywhere. Your poor father was exhausted; I drove him home hours ago. Where on earth have you been? You knew he'd be too tired to stay long."

"Oh, God, it's Mum," Bethany muttered. We stood up, hand in hand, turning to face her.

At first Angela just looked confused. Then her face changed, hardened, when she got a proper look at me. Her mouth opened slightly, as if she couldn't believe what she was seeing.

"What the bloody hell is he doing here? What do you think you're doing?" Angela spoke in a low, furious hiss. Actually much more scary than shouting. If she hadn't been so worried how it would look to other people, she would have raked my face to shreds with her expensively manicured fingernails.

"Don't talk to her like that," I said, sharply.

"You stupid girl, Bethany. I can't believe you've actually done this!" Angela hissed. She was spitting mad. "Do you have any idea how upset Daddy is going to be? How dare you? This boy is a bad influence, and we've made our feelings clear. My God, I just don't know how you can be so selfish – and *stupid*. Especially at the moment."

"Don't bring Dad into it!" Bethany shouted. I'd never seen her look so angry. She really did have guts. "It was *your* idea I shouldn't see Jack. Not his. Wasn't it?"

"That's enough! All you care about is yourself, young lady. It makes me sick, absolutely sick. Your father deserves better than this. You're just making everything worse."

Bethany looked as if she'd been kicked. Her shoulders dropped, the light went out of her face, as if some invisible vampire had sucked the life from her body.

"That's not fair," I said. "You can't blame Bethany because he's ill. It's not her fault."

Angela turned to me. Her face was still twisted with anger. "Right, come with me. I'm taking you home, Jack. We'll see what your parents have got to say about this, shall we?"

"Mum, *don't*!" Bethany's eyes were bright, as if she was trying not to cry.

"Be quiet!" snapped Angela. "I've heard enough from you for one evening. I hope you realize this puts an end to your

Glastonbury plans, Bethany. You clearly can't be trusted. And to think I was prepared to give you another chance after what you did last weekend. You must think I came down in the last shower of rain. Come with me this minute, both of you – I've absolutely had enough."

For a moment I thought about legging it – there was nothing I wanted less than to get into a car with that woman, but at the same time I didn't want to leave Bethany to face her mother alone. By the time they'd dropped me off, maybe Angela would have cooled down a bit.

"It's all right," I said to Bethany. "Don't worry."

"Jack, I—" Tears slid silently down her face.

"Not another word," said Angela, in this really evil voice.

We followed her to the car in silence.

It was the worst car journey of my entire life. I had to sit in the front and Bethany on her own in the back as if I was some kind of potential rapist who might attack at any moment. Luckily, I'd started feeling a bit less trippy, but I was still pretty hammered and, by then, really horribly wide awake; I didn't dare look across at Angela in the driver's seat. Bethany sat behind me; I felt like I could hear the beating of her heart. It was killing me being so close, yet not touching.

Angela drove properly badly – stalling at the traffic lights outside town, revving the engine too hard, taking corners really fast. I was terrified she might hit something. Her jaw was set totally rigid; her hands gripped the steering wheel like horrible claws. God, I hated her. How could Bethany have such a hideous mother?

And again, as soon as I saw our house, I knew something was wrong. For one thing, a light was on in the basement: I could see the glow striking up through the wrought iron grid, hitting street level. Someone was in the kitchen. And there was a big, shiny car parked in the visitor's permit space next to our wreck of a Ford. OK, so it could have belonged to anyone down our road.

It looked like a hire car, though.

Angela pulled up outside the house so suddenly we were all jerked forwards in our seats.

"Mum, be careful!" Bethany gasped.

Angela ignored her, just slammed out of the car and came around to open my door. Shit. She was blatantly coming in. This was not good. Really not.

When we got to the porch, Angela reached for the bell but I got my keys out before she had the chance to ring.

I pushed the door open.

"Listen," I said, trying to sound reasonable, "it's three in the morning—"

"I'm aware of that!" Angela shoved past me like she owned the place. The kitchen light was still on, sending a yellow glow up the basement stairs. "I suggest you wake your mother, Jack. If you don't, I will. I'd like a word with her. Now. I'll wait down here."

I ignored that, though, followed her downstairs. Angela

opened the kitchen door and I nearly died of shock.

My dad was sitting at the table, reading a paperback copy of *The I-Ching*.

He looked up, putting down the book. There was a glass of whisky on the table but it hadn't reached his eyes. They were clear, cold. The mirror of mine. The mirror of Owen's. The mirror of Herod's.

"What the hell is going on?" Dad asked.

It was a fair enough question. I was dressed as a pirate, obviously quite smashed, and Angela was still in her tight gold Cleopatra costume.

Angela was just standing there, mouth slightly open. "Who are you?" she asked. I thought of Bethany, alone in the car, wondering what was happening.

"I might ask you the same question," said Dad, and if I hadn't been so scared I would have laughed. She looked like a complete idiot now.

"I need to speak to Jack's parents, that's all." The hard expression on Angela's face softened slightly. *She bloody fancies him*, I thought, disgusted. *Jesus Christ*.

"Well," Dad gave me a really scary look, "I'm his father. What's the problem?"

Oh, this was just charming. I hadn't seen him for two years and now he was looking at me like I'd crawled out from under a rock.

I couldn't stop myself. "Right," I said. "As if you care."

Dad's eyes narrowed, but before anyone had time to speak,

the door flew open behind us and Mum came in, followed by Louis. They were still dressed, though Mum was wearing jeans and a cardigan – not the stuff she'd gone out in earlier.

"Jack, where have you been?" Mum demanded, furious. "I obviously can't trust you at all." She turned to Angela, looking her up and down, taking in the gold lamé dress, the massive necklace, all that black eye make-up. "What on earth is going on?"

"Your son gatecrashed a party," Angela cut in before I had the chance to speak. "I found him there with Bethany. I thought I'd asked you to keep him away from my daughter!"

"Oh, Jack, you idiot," Louis said.

Mum took a deep breath, obviously trying to stay calm. "Thank you very much for bringing Jack home, Angela. I'm extremely sorry. I really am. Now, if you don't mind, it's very late."

"I suggest you learn to control your child." Angela gave me one last evil look, then turned and walked out, shutting the kitchen door behind her.

Mum stood completely still, arms folded, till she'd gone.

I felt like I'd been thrown into a pit of snakes.

"Jack, how could you do this to me?" Mum burst into tears.

I looked from her to Dad and back again. My head was spinning. "What's he doing here?" I demanded. My heart thudded harder and harder. I turned to Dad. "What do you want?"

Dad stood up. "You need to watch your mouth."

"You can't talk to me like that!" I snapped, so angry I couldn't stop myself. Who did he think he was?

"That's enough!" Mum said. "Edward, you can't blame him for wondering." She turned back to me. "Your father is here to look for Herod."

"Seems a good thing I came back, judging by the state of Jack." Dad looked at me, pointedly. I probably stank of booze, but it was like he somehow just knew about the mushrooms, too. "Or are you just happy for the whole thing to happen again, Caroline? Wasn't one son's wasted life enough?"

"That's completely out of order," Louis shouted. Everyone stared. I had literally never heard Louis raise his voice before.

Dad just ignored him. "Your mother called my cell phone not long after I arrived at Heathrow—"

"Louis and I found a message from the police when we got back from supper," Mum said. She was crying. Louis handed her a piece of kitchen towel. She wiped her eyes, smearing mascara everywhere. "They'd found a body—"

A body.

Herod.

I closed my eyes and in my mind I saw Herod's hands, clay-stained, fingers moving quick, delicate around the clay – hardly seeming to touch it as he formed a curled-up autumn leaf that looked like it would float if dropped.

Louis put his arm around Mum's shoulders.

"We went to the mortuary together," Mum said, speaking

slowly. "Your father and I. Louis stayed here. The police said we could wait till the morning, that some families prefer to take a bit of time, but I couldn't bear it. And all the way there, two hours it must have been, I couldn't stop thinking, *Please let it not be him. Anyone else's child but mine—* We've only just got back."

"Was it him?" I sounded a lot calmer than I felt. I gripped the Aga rail harder; my head was swimming – I wanted to sink down on my knees.

Why couldn't she just say it? *Herod's dead.*

"No." Mum's voice was flat. "No, it was someone else. He'd been in the water a few days, poor boy, but even so I could easily tell it wasn't Herod, thank God. Thank God."

Relief gushed through my body in a great, cool wave.

Dad said nothing, just carried on looking at me with total disgust. I was getting more and more angry by the second, so furious I actually felt totally sober. Who the hell was he to judge?

"We got back to find you were gone." Mum's voice was too high now, ragged-sounding – she was pretty close to the edge, and I started to feel really scared. I'd never seen her like that before. "It's unbelievable that you would go off like this again when you know Herod's missing, when you were supposed to be here in case the phone rang and you knew that we're worried sick as it is."

I took a long, steadying breath. "I'd do the same again to see Bethany."

"Jack, don't be an idiot," Louis said. "Don't make this any worse."

Mum shook her head. "Bethany's parents made it clear enough, didn't they? What's the matter with you? I don't want that woman coming around here again, Jack. Stay away from Bethany."

"You can't make me," I said. "You can't."

"We're not the only ones who are concerned," Louis said quickly, before Mum had the chance to answer me. "There was a message from Mr Trelawney, too – he called on Friday afternoon. He's worried about you."

I had a bad feeling about that twenty quid note. *Trelawney can't know you took it. Even if he guessed, he's got no way of proving it.* I knew Jono and Sammy would never grass me up: Sammy because he's loyal, Jono because he's not stupid. Neither of them had a sensible explanation for being in Trelawney's classroom at midnight on a Monday.

"What's going on, Jack?" Dad said. "What the hell have you got yourself into?"

"Why don't you all just get off my back?" I yelled. I turned to Mum and Louis. "If you two hadn't gone along with Bethany's bitch of a mother we wouldn't have to sneak around. Why can't you leave us alone instead of trying to guilt-trip me? This has nothing to do with Herod. It's my life, not his."

"Jack—" said my dad, getting up, walking over.

And suddenly I couldn't take it any more.

"It's got nothing to do with you, either!" I shouted. "You can't just *walk in here* and look at me like I'm a piece of shit. What's the problem, anyway. What's it to you all of a sudden? Do you even care about Herod? Or are you just scared someone might find out you abandoned your kids?"

"Shut up," said my dad, very calmly, and slapped me right across the face.

It hurt. It really hurt. I couldn't believe he'd hit me. He'd actually hit me. It stung like hell, as if someone had held a hot iron against my skin, but I said nothing, just stared at him, hoping he could feel my hatred – because that's what it was. I hated him.

"Edward!" Mum snapped.

"You're useless!" I shouted at him. "Just useless. You're never here, you never even phone. Maybe if you'd ever bothered Herod wouldn't be like he is. You can't just turn up now and start acting like you're God."

I turned to walk out but Dad grabbed me by the arm. "My car is outside," Dad said to me, making an obvious effort to control his anger. "Please go and get in it."

"I'm not going anywhere with you," I laughed. "You must be fucking joking. I mean, what gives you the right?"

Dad just ignored me.

"Let's keep this in perspective, Edward, OK?" Louis said. "We've all had a terrible evening, but to be fair Jack didn't know what was going on."

Dad nodded towards the phone on the counter. "Feel free

to call a lawyer, Caroline. It's pretty clear you're not handling this."

Mum and Louis stared at him. Call a lawyer?

And by "this" did he mean me? As if I was some kind of project one of his employees had screwed up?

How had everything got so badly out of control?

"Don't be ridiculous," Mum said. "Jack, go and get some sleep. We'll talk about this tomorrow."

"Get in the car," Dad told me again, not paying her any attention whatsoever.

"You can't take him!" Mum's voice rang out in a shriek. "You can't turn up here and take him! You don't deserve to have any bloody children."

"You're becoming hysterical, Caroline," said my dad, and, glancing at me, he pointed towards the door. An unspoken order. Who did he think he was? Adolf Hitler? Oh, please.

Mum, Louis and Dad all started talking at once but I couldn't make sense of what they were saying; I was hardly listening. My ears were still ringing; I'd never heard Mum shout like that before, more like a scared child than an adult.

Slowly, I walked to the door, letting them think I was heading for the car. There were plenty of options between there and the house. I know this town like the back of my hand. I could go to Sammy's. Yvonne would definitely let me stay. All I had to do was make Dad think I was toeing the line, then get away.

"Wait," Louis said. "Why don't we just talk this through calmly in the morning. We're all tired."

Dad glanced at the kitchen clock. It was quarter to four. "It is the morning," he said.

I ran for the door. Mum and Louis both shouted my name at once.

Dad caught up with me a few yards from the car, grabbed my arm. "Just get in." He wasn't even out of breath. He was like some kind of Californian yoga-posing beansprout-eating hippy Terminator. He shoved me into the front seat and as I sat down the exhaustion hit me. The smell of air freshener and new leather made me feel sick. Mum and Dad were now arguing in low, furious voices in the street outside.

Louis came over to the car and I wound down the window. "Well, this time you've really done it." He patted me on the arm. "You absolute bloody idiot."

I wished Louis could know how grateful I felt that he was there, letting it all wash over him, calm and sarcastic as ever. He made everything seem less weird, less scary. My face was still burning. "Do I have to go? I really, really don't want to."

Louis nodded, speaking quickly. "For now, yes, I think you do. But listen, don't worry, OK? Your father's staying at his place in Oxford – it's not far, is it? He's flown all the way from Japan. No one's at their best after nine hours on a plane, even if it's business class. He's very concerned about Herod. And you." Louis let those last two words hang in the air.

What about Bethany? How was I going to see Bethany if I was in Oxford?

I sat back in the seat, nodding. "OK." But it wasn't OK. Not at all.

Louis smiled and patted me on the arm again. "It'll be all right," he said. "We'll have a sensible conversation about all this tomorrow."

I knew he was lying.

FIFTEEN

I woke up thinking of Bethany; a tangle of dark hair, a smile, silver glitter shining all over her face, the scent of heat and lemons. My head hurt. A dull, sore ache.

I was in the wrong place. A clean, featureless white room. I was lying between sheets that smelt of fabric conditioner. Light slanted in between thick dark curtains.

Oxford. My father's house in Oxford. My face still stung, very faintly. He'd hit me.

It was quiet. I remembered that from before, a long time ago. I could hear birdsong outside and, bizarrely, a cow. The house backed on to Port Meadow, a green spread of fields. When we came to see Radiohead play – me, Sammy, Jono, Georgie Hicks and Amanda – we'd sat on the grass with our cider, only a few hundred yards from here. There were cows then, too. In the middle of a city. Weird. I sneaked a look at this place then, at Dad's house, but the windows had just stared back at me, blank, giving nothing away.

I've only been here once before, when I was about four, not long after Mum and Dad split up. So he'd kept the place. I suppose he could afford it – houses all over the place. I tried to piece together what clues this pale, clean room might give me about my father. What advantages over him, if any. I really didn't know him at all.

He'd come back. My father. Goes to show you should always be careful what you wish for. You might just get it.

I had no way of knowing what the time was.

I squeezed my eyes closed against the light. Oh, God. It was Sunday. In five days, Bethany and I were meant to be getting on a train with Jono and Sammy to Castle Cary. Glastonbury. Angela would blatantly try and stop us. Would Mum even let me go now I'd been caught at that stupid party?

And what about Dad?

I just wished I could call Bethany, but it was too dangerous. I had no way of telling who would pick up the phone.

What was she thinking about now? A paranoid, niggling thought crept into my mind. What if she was only using me to get back at her mother? *Am I a weapon?* I thought.

I think I'm falling in love with you. That's what she'd said. Bethany had more courage than I did. The truth of it was I'd loved her since the moment she stepped on the train with me in her pink silk dress and black wellingtons, fake flowers in her hair, smiling. Brave.

I lay on the bed, staring up at the white ceiling, and laughed at myself.

What are you thinking, you idiot? You're practically under house arrest. Stop worrying about how you and Bethany are getting to Glastonbury: how the hell are you going to get out of this mess?

Still wearing my pirate outfit, I eased myself off the bed and lurched to the door. Every muscle in my body screamed and shrieked.

I waited before opening the door, listening. Now I remembered being escorted up more than one flight of stairs, a dimly lit corridor, someone pushing me along. That must have been him. My father. I wondered what had been going through his mind, thinking about the last time I'd seen him, nearly two years ago. It had been in London, just before the Easter holidays. I got a day off school. I went down with Mum on the train, but I met Dad alone. We had lunch in a restaurant with no prices listed on the menu, near the Apple headquarters where he'd been going for meetings. He asked the normal questions about school and gave me a hundred quid, all according to the usual rules of engagement.

Why should he suddenly care?

If Herod had just bothered to call, none of this would have happened. All right, Mum would still have been angry about the party, but the fact she'd spent the entire evening in a mortuary hadn't exactly helped.

Thanks a lot, mate, I thought. *It's bad enough that Mum thinks I'm going to lose the plot if I even look at a spliff.*

If Mum and Louis hadn't come back from France in a huge panic because Herod was missing, they might have even taken my side against Bethany's bitch of a mother, too.

But what if Herod hadn't called because he couldn't? There was no way of ignoring the question. If the Creature had come back, Herod might be anywhere, doing anything. What if he'd tried to hurt someone? That's what everyone said he'd done last time. Maybe now he really had. He could already have been involuntarily sectioned, like before, held in some awful hospital ward, blood pumped full of drugs that made him shake and dribble.

I couldn't figure out why Dad was doing this to me. It was Herod he'd come looking for – and he'd only done that because Herod out of the Peace Centre meant that a cog had come loose in the machine. A situation that needed to be managed. Dealt with.

Come on Herod, I thought. *Just call someone. Let them know you're OK, and we can all go back to normal.*

I stood holding the door handle. It didn't look good. It was over a week since Herod's friend Andrea had phoned Sabine in Paris. I pictured Louis' tiny, grey-haired mother frowning as she put down the telephone. Picking up the receiver again, dialling.

But how would Herod even know that Andrea had called Sabine, and that we had all descended into a full-on panic? He'd probably got no idea we even knew he'd left.

I thought of Andrea – her long frizzy hair, the annoying chumminess. A bit too eager to please. *Anyone for carrot cake? Tea? I'm making one.* Hanging round when really she should have left us all to it. Herod smiling, saying, *I think we're all good. Thanks, though, Andy.*

But it didn't matter what little stories I told myself. The truth was we had no idea why Herod had disappeared, or where he might have gone.

I felt as if I was standing on the edge of a cliff, ready to jump. I pushed open the door.

The house was quiet, the hall floorboards had been polished: butter-yellow and shining, they gave off a faint scent of lavender. The walls were lined with bookcases. I stopped and looked at the spines. *Theory of Economics. The Essence of Being.* Thirty-year-old university textbooks, left lining the hallways of a house nobody came to. Further on, a wooden African mask stared at me from the wall. Now I could hear people talking. I stopped before I reached the top of the stairs, letting out a long breath. Just the radio.

When I found the kitchen – all gleaming stainless steel – I realized the house wasn't empty, after all. A slight, wiry woman with caramel-coloured hair lay on the sofa, reading a newspaper. Slowly, she lowered it and stared at me, mouth slightly open. She wore all black. There was something feline about the way she moved. Her bare arms were lean, muscled.

"You must be Jack. You can't be the other one. You're too young." She looked bored.

And you must be one of his many girlfriends, I thought, but said nothing.

The woman shrugged, turning back to her paper. "There's coffee in the pot. Make yourself at home." She didn't introduce herself. She just assumed I knew who she was.

Great. Thanks for reminding me that although the man who owns this house is my father, I'm here as a guest. Or is it as a prisoner?

I poured coffee into a cup from a stainless steel jug, drank it black and sugarless. My head was getting clearer every second. I wondered how long they'd been together.

It was one in the afternoon, according to the digital clock on the stove. What was the scene like at Bethany's? It wasn't going to be pretty. I wished I was with her somewhere far away from all this. Where could we go? I just wanted to escape with her.

"Where is he?" I asked.

Dad's girlfriend put down her paper, stared at me again, a slight look of disbelief crossing her face.

"London," she said, as if I should have known. "There's a list of homeless shelters."

I put down the coffee cup and walked out of the kitchen.

SIXTEEN

It was pretty weird, having a teacher make you a cup of tea.
But Trelawney did it anyway.

"Three sugars." He put the striped mug on the desk in
front of me and sighed. "Oh, for the days I didn't have to
watch my love handles."

Nice.

I nodded my thanks, uncomfortable in the new clothes.
Dad's girlfriend – Alicia, apparently – had unloaded a pile of
glossy plastic bags onto my bed late on Sunday afternoon.

"He asked me to get you these. I had to guess your size
but I doubt I'm wrong, darling." The kind of person who
calls everyone "darling" even if they'd rather see you run over
by an articulated lorry.

I think that was the moment I felt the first real stab of

fear. There were a lot of clothes in those bags – expensive, boring stuff I'd never normally wear. *How long am I meant to be staying here?* I thought.

"So," Trelawney went on, and then stopped. It was half nine on Monday morning. Everyone else was in Geography and possibly for the first time ever I wished I was, too. "Don't worry about not being in uniform today. Or the lack of homework – till tomorrow, anyway. I've told the rest of the staff you're staying with your dad…"

A silent question lingered in the air. And there wasn't even time to throw a few clothes into a bag? Pick up some books?

"Anyway," Mr Trelawney went on, "when I spoke to your father this morning he said a car would come to collect you at the end of the school day." He frowned. "I gather he won't be here himself." Trelawney shook his head and I could tell he didn't like it any more than I did. "Listen, Jack, last week I left some money in my desk. It's gone."

Suddenly, I felt totally cold.

"And there's something else as well," Trelawney went on. "Mrs Hannay has been looking everywhere for her new television, but it seems to have completely vanished from the school building. Apparently there aren't any signs of a break-in. It's all very strange."

He didn't actually say it: *You took my money. You took Mrs Hannay's TV.* But he knew. He knew.

Stay cool, I told myself. *Just stay cool. He's got no proof.*

"It's been a long time since I've had money stolen by a

student," Trelawney went on. "Actually, the last time it happened, it was your brother, Herod."

"He was sick," I said. "He didn't know what he was doing."

Trelawney nodded, slowly, never taking his eyes off me. "Are you sure you're all right, Jack? All this business with your father must be quite disruptive."

It was a warning. I understood. *Do it again and I'll tell your parents.* He wanted me to talk but I didn't have anything to say. Not to him: there was only one person I wanted and she wasn't there.

I said all I needed to when Jono and Sammy found me at break. Trelawney had let me go just as they were leaving Geography; we went straight to the back field, sat down beneath the trees by the far fence, and Sammy gave me a fag. I smoked for a few moments in silence, heart still pounding, and then told them what had happened. Everything.

They stared at me. At last Jono said, "Are you serious? Your dad just, like, *forced* you to go with him? That's like something out of medieval times. We couldn't find you anywhere. We did look."

"We shouldn't have left without you," Sammy muttered. "I knew we shouldn't. You should've come over to mine. Bloody hell. I can't believe your dad did that. What a tosser." He stared down at the grass. "I hope your brother's OK, Jack. That's pretty dark, the police and everything. I can't believe your mum had to look at an actual dead body."

I blew out a cloud, dizzy with the nicotine rush. "Look, I don't even care about my dad, OK? He'll get bored of looking for Herod soon and I'll go home, and it'll all be cool."

"I mean, what are the police even doing?" Sammy went on.

"Herod's an adult," I said. "It's not like a kid going missing, is it? It's not illegal. The cops searched the place he lives, the gardens and stuff, but no one's out in a helicopter looking for him."

Jono's eyes suddenly widened. "What about Glastonbury?" he blurted. "There's no way your dad's going to let you go, is there?"

"Look," Sammy said, "maybe my mum could call him, tell him you'll be working and stuff—"

I shook my head, impatient. None of this was important. Dad might have his opinion about whether I was going to Glastonbury or not, but that was all it was – an opinion. I wasn't going to let his opinion make any difference to what I actually did.

"It's Bethany I'm bothered about," I said, "I need to know what happened." I told them about the horrible scene with her mother.

"That's not good," Sammy said. "Bethany's mum'll be watching her like a hawk now. How's she going to come with us? Do you reckon she'll get away with it? Mum's going to be pissed off if she's got to mess around with the rota."

"I'm going over there at lunchtime." I sucked in the last drag of my cigarette and ground out the stub. "St Agnes's."

Jono shook his head. "You'll never get a pass out. No way. Not with all this going on. Trelawney won't sign it off. It's not like you can just walk in to St Agnes's, either. There's those gates, too."

But Sammy had already got it. "You're going to do it anyway, aren't you?"

"Oh, God," Jono said. "Just don't tell us anything else. Don't even say a word."

"Don't worry," I told him kindly. "What you don't know can't hurt you."

It was pretty amazing, really, but I walked out of school at lunchtime and that was it. No one tried to stop me. I wasn't even in uniform – which was like a massive arrow pointing over my head – but nobody noticed. I just left. St Agnes's is in the middle of town, in what used to be a nunnery – we call it the Virgin Megastore. It's set back from the road, a sprawling timber-framed building behind iron gates with a load of shiny new sports halls out the back on the playing fields. The gates were locked, obviously, and the sweeping lawn leading up to the front door was dotted with groups of glossy-haired girls in burgundy skirts and blazers, sitting on the grass in peaceful little groups, or wandering around arm in arm. It looked more like a stately home than a school. It's amazing how civilized girls are. Everything was so calm and peaceful.

There was a bin just next to the gate. Standing on top of it, I climbed over the wall and dropped down into the hallowed grounds of St Agnes's School for Girls. I had, I estimated, about five minutes before a teacher saw me or one of the Virgins panicked and called one.

I walked up to the first group of girls I saw and said, "Where's Bethany Jones?"

They couldn't have been any older than twelve. They just stared at me, looking really freaked out, till one of them said, "She and Amelia normally hang out under the cherry trees. Just over there."

I followed her gaze. There she was. Bethany. Running towards me, black hair loose everywhere. Watched by two hundred schoolgirls, we held each other as if no one else was there.

"Jack, Jack, Jack," she whispered into my ear. She looked tired, dark rings beneath her eyes. "What are you doing? They'll tell my parents and that really can't happen now—"

I thought she was talking about her mum and the party, but she wasn't.

"I'm not staying," I said. "Come on, let's get out of here. Just for a few hours." I was past the point of caring what happened next.

"No, listen, it's my dad. We thought he'd just overdone it going to the party, but it's not that. He's not well. He's gone back to hospital again. A different one this time – in London." Her voice sounded thin, brittle.

She wasn't leaving.

Her dad was going to die.

"Don't worry," I said. "Don't." I wasn't going to promise her that everything would be all right, though. I just held her tighter. She had it worse than me. She loved her dad and he was dying. I only hated mine.

"I must see you. I'll come to yours tonight. I'll sneak out."

"You can't." And I told her what had happened, what my dad had done.

Bethany started to cry. "He can't do that to you. It's not fair." I knew she wasn't really talking about my father when she said that, but her own. "It's really not fair. When am I going to see you, then?"

I smiled, even though I was holding her close to my chest and she couldn't see. "Glastonbury," I told her. "At the Veggie Café, the Green Fields. Eleven on Friday night. Don't be late."

"All right," she whispered. "I'll be there." She smiled, even though she was crying. "You know what? Dad actually persuaded Mum to let me go. He said, 'Because you're only young once.'"

I smiled at her. "He's a really nice guy. But whatever happens," I went on, "I promise I won't leave you. OK?"

"OK," she said, still crying. "OK."

Then the shouting started, and she pushed me away, even though her face was covered in tears. "That's Miss Matthews. You should go. Run, Jack!"

"I love you," I said.

Bethany looked me dead in the eye. "I know."

I turned and I walked to the gate.

* * *

I got back into school through the broken fence on the back field just as the bell rang for the end of lunchtime. It was a victory, but it didn't feel like one. I walked into the classroom like a blind man, bumped into someone who shoved me, and I didn't even register who it was. I stared into the distance, seeing nothing, till some sixth form guy stuck his head round the door and said to Mr Hawking, "Sir, Mr Trelawney wants to see Jack MacNamara."

So he knew. Someone had seen me after all.

"You're really in it," the sixth former said, leaving me outside the Art Block. "They were going insane in Mrs Watts' office."

I didn't reply. Trelawney came banging out of his classroom in a proper rage, "We just had a call from St Agnes's saying you were seen in the grounds at lunchtime. What is all this about?" He was really pissed off. I'd never seen him like that before. He was practically snarling at me.

What did he expect, an answer? *The girl I love is there and I had to see her, Mr Trelawney.* Yeah, right. I stood and stared at him, silent.

What Trelawney said next left me feeling pretty sick.

"I'm afraid to say, Jack, that I called your parents. Both of them."

I closed my eyes a moment, cold with horror. Had he told them about the TV? The money?

"Look," Trelawney went on, sounding less angry now he'd

delivered his coup de grâce. "I don't really see that I had much of a choice. You might as well have just asked me to do it. Sometimes I wonder if you use your brain at all, Jack. Which is a shame because you're one of the few people in this school with a really fine mind – and I'm including the teachers. What's the matter with you, Jack?" He shook his head. "Listen, your father will be here at the end of the day and your mother wants you to phone her at work. You'd better come in."

So Trelawney herded me into the classroom, past the bug-eyed Year Eights staring at me like I'd just grown a second head, and into the little room at the back. There was another desk in there among sheets of plywood leaning against the wall. Someone had carved great tumbling piles of falling leaves into the plywood. They glowed golden in the flickering electric light, and I realized this was Trelawney's own work. *Poor guy*, I remember thinking. *Getting a load of snotty kids to draw oranges when he's got more talent in one fingernail.*

There was a copy of Saturday's *Guardian* magazine on the desk. *Alicia Sykes: A Dancer for Our Times. For more than twenty years a prima ballerina with the National Ballet, now she devotes her time to avant-garde choreography.* I couldn't help staring at the picture. I recognized the dancer; I even recognized the hi-tech kitchen they'd photographed her in, complete with cosy props in the background: jars of home-made marmalade (imported from somewhere), bunches of flowers. It was Dad's girlfriend, Alicia. Dad's kitchen. Their kitchen. Their important, busy life in which I was an unwelcome guest.

I stared down at my hand as I picked up the phone on the desk and it was as if it belonged to someone else. It was the same speaking to Mum, like I was listening to another person do it.

"I'm not even angry with you now," she said, sounding exhausted. I knew straight away Trelawney hadn't mentioned the money, and silently thanked him. "Actually, I'm just really worried, Jack. You seem utterly out of touch with anyone's feelings except your own. I don't like Bethany's mother but she was very upset about you going to that party. Her poor husband, too—"

"I know about Bethany's dad, OK. I know he's really ill. But not being allowed to see each other just makes it all worse for Bethany. Her mum's totally overreacting."

"I don't blame her!" Mum replied, sharply. "She can't exactly be thinking straight, can she, with her husband in that condition. For the record, I don't agree with her: I think you and Bethany should see each other if you want to, but it's not my decision. If Bethany's mother doesn't like it, that's it. That family must be going through a living nightmare at the moment. The fact is you shouldn't have gone to that party, Jack, or her school. And you know it, too. I know you do." A pause. "How are things at your father's?"

"Fine."

I heard Mum draw in a deep breath. "Look, I'm not going to storm up to school this afternoon and cause a drama. It's important your father feels he has some influence with you.

He'll collect you at the end of the day." She sighed. I hate it when she speaks like an *Idiot's Guide to Psychology*. "Since he's clearly feeling the need to be involved at the moment."

She carried on talking but I couldn't take it in.

"Mum," I eventually interrupted, "what about Glastonbury? I'm meant to be getting the train on Friday, aren't I?"

A pause. "We'll talk about that later."

It didn't sound good. Well, not that it made any difference whatsoever. I was going anyway. This time, they'd know where I was. It wasn't like going off to that party without telling anyone – or going missing. It was more of a disagreement. They needn't be worried about me like they were about Herod. They knew where I was going, and they'd be idiots not to figure out who I was with.

It wasn't my fault if they didn't like it.

I'd just put the phone down when Trelawney came in and said to me, "I don't trust you an inch, MacNamara. You can bloody well stay in the classroom till the bell goes."

He sat me down at the back, told the Year Eights to stop staring and that I wasn't much of an example, and gave me a pile of seashells to draw. So I sat there through a whole double lesson, drawing seashells in charcoal, staring out of the window at the teachers' car park and wondering where all this was going to end. I wished I was down by the sea with Bethany, throwing shells back into the curling waves, even in the rain.

What was it Mum used to say? *If wishes were fishes, there'd be no space in the sea.*

SEVENTEEN

OK, so I'll admit that by half three I was pretty scared. Dad had lamped me once; what if he did it again? At school. Social death. But you know what? In the end, he didn't even come himself. She did. Alicia. A Dancer for Our Times. Whatever. He didn't even bother. Mr Trelawney walked me to the car. Alicia was lounging in the driver's seat, sunglasses on. Trelawney must have been reading the *Guardian* like I had but made no sign that he recognized her. At least he's got some style. I could feel the disapproval coming off him in waves.

"You're really quite a handful, aren't you?" Alicia said as I got into the car. She gave a stupid fake sigh, as if she was acting in a play. "I shouldn't have expected less from one of Edward's sons." She was making it sound as if she knew us: bullshit.

The worst thing about Dad not coming was the arrogance. He knew I would go with Alicia because he knew I was slightly afraid of him. It was true. That's the scary thing about my father: he knows what you are thinking; he reads people. It's why he's rich, and it's why he has the kind of girlfriend who appears in the *Guardian* weekend magazine.

So I wasn't exactly in the mood for a cosy chit-chat with Alicia. I turned to her. It was about time we got a few things straight.

"Listen," I said, "I don't like this any more than you do, OK?"

Alicia rolled her eyes, pushed the sunglasses back onto her nose and let out the clutch. As we pulled away, she turned to me and said, "Your father and I have guests this evening. The least you can do is not embarrass him with your silly little teenage moods, OK?"

Obviously, I didn't bother to answer.

By the time we reached Oxford it was late. The traffic's bad in rush hour and the Dancer for Our Times was getting increasingly annoyed as the snaking line of cars and buses inched around the ring road.

Alicia stalked off upstairs the minute we got back and for a moment I stood alone in the kitchen, wondering what the hell to do. What was Dad going to say when he got home? I started feeling sick in the pit of my belly. The thing was, I really didn't know how he might react. In the end, I went from room to room, looking for somewhere with a TV. I just wanted to zone out. There wasn't one. In a large sitting room with windows overlooking the meadow, I found a projector and a screen that pulled down from the ceiling like a roller-blind. There was a collection of films but, weirdly, they were mainly French – the same kind of stuff Mum and Louis have at home, with a whole load of meaningful silences, kinky hairdressers and not a lot else.

I left that room through a double door and found myself in a library lined with bookshelves. Rugs covered the floor from wall to wall. The air felt thick, syrupy. Early evening light shone in, tinted green by overgrown vine-leaves clustering around a window which faced on to a small gravel garden surrounded with iron railings, all of which were probably maintained at great expense by someone Dad had never even met. I looked at a few of the books but they were mostly old with leather spines, thin yellowing pages and cramped lettering.

In one corner, there was a glass cabinet taller than me containing nothing but a single glass shelf and a porcelain bowl coated with a blueish glaze.

"Ah. You found the Tang dynasty bowl. One of your father's favourite pieces, I believe. It's over one thousand years old." I hadn't even heard anyone come in. I turned around slowly, not wanting whoever it was to know they'd given me the fear. There was a guy standing in the door-way – someone I'd never seen before, although the voice was familiar. He smiled, showing very white teeth. His hair was short, blonde and glossy. He looked like a well-kept Labrador. "I hope I didn't startle you. I'm Marcus Stuvesyant – your father's personal assistant. We've spoken on the phone a few times, I think." He smiled. "We've had kind of a long day but Ed's ready to see you now." Marcus walked closer, holding out one hand for me to shake, still smiling. "It's nice to meet you at last, Jack."

He was probably about the same age as Owen and Herod but, oh, Lordy, Marcus here had taken a different path through the dangerous jungle of life. High-end university in the States probably followed by building orphanages in the Third World, then a tasty and no doubt eye-wateringly well-paid job as personal slave to my dear father. But then Marcus seemed like a nice guy. I shook his hand, suddenly feeling like I didn't want to come across as a brat.

"You, too." I smiled back. "You'd better lead the way – I haven't got a clue where anything is around here."

Just to ram home the point that although "Ed" was my dad, he really didn't know me; I didn't even know my way around his house.

Marcus smoothed over a look of surprise and grinned at me. "These old British places are like warrens sometimes. This one's eighteenth century, Alicia tells me. Wonderful."

"Yes," I said. "It's great, isn't it?" I can turn it on when I have to, but in my head I was counting to ten, trying to control my irritation. It was starting to get on my nerves, being treated like some kind of employee who'd stepped out of line. If Dad wanted to speak to me, why couldn't he just come and find me like any normal person instead of issuing a summons as if he was some kind of lord and master from the Victorian times. But I kept a lid on it and followed the blonde Labrador through the library and down a corridor lined with creepy Japanese-looking masks.

We came to a set of heavy carved double doors painted white, and Marcus laid one smooth hand on my arm. He was pretty well built but you could tell it was all from the gym. His hands were so clean, the fingernails perfectly round. "Just in here." He spoke in a soft voice as if we were in a church. "You'd better knock. He's working." And Marcus moved silently away across polished floorboards like a ghost.

Knock? Yeah, right.

I opened the door and went in. At first, my dad didn't even seem to notice I was there. He was sitting behind a glass desk, which should have looked weird with all the old Indian rugs and dark furniture, but it didn't. It looked cool. An Anglepoise lamp shed a circle of clear light over a sheaf of A1 – thick, heavy cartridge paper. Creamy white. He had been drawing in ink and pastels – some bright sharp colours, others paler and more muted. It was all abstract, intricate and tightly woven – one shape leading into another, an endless pattern.

Dad glanced up and I held my breath for a second: he looked just like Herod.

"Jack," he said, "I'm glad you're here. I need to talk to you.

First of all, I owe you an apology: I shouldn't have hit you yesterday. There's no excuse. It was a bad night and I lost my temper."

I shrugged. This totally wasn't what I'd expected. "It's OK." What was he doing? I couldn't take my eyes off the swirl of psychedelic colour. Before I could stop myself, forgetting I was meant to hate his guts, I said, "What are you drawing? Music or numbers?"

"So you remember that," Dad said. "Both, actually. It's an idea I've had. For musicians. You know, in a few years anyone with a decent computer will be able to have their own recording studio at home. Mixing, retracking, adjusting levels. All just by downloading the right software. You're artistic, though – right?"

"Kind of. I'm not that good."

"If that was your work in Caroline's kitchen, you're lying. Those sketches of a cat were very skilled," Dad said, unsmiling. A barrier between us had moved away like a sliding window.

I was about to answer but the phone rang, breaking the spell. Dad picked it up immediately, frowning slightly. His eyes flickered to the window; this one faced on to the meadow. A group of copper-coloured cows meandered past. High above the trees, a single bird hovered. I was forgotten: all Dad's attention was focused on the phone call now.

"Thanks for calling. OK. OK. I'd be grateful if you could do that, yes." He put the phone down, scribbled something on his paper, and sat looking out of the window for a moment. I couldn't read the expression on his face at all. He turned towards me but it was as if I wasn't even in the room; he didn't see me, just leaned forwards, elbows on the desk, resting his head in his hands a moment.

"Who was it?" I asked, feeling like an intruder, as if I'd witnessed something I shouldn't have. Something private. What had it been? Fear? Despair? None of this was turning out like I'd thought.

"The duty manager at Centrepoint in London." Dad's voice had changed, hardened. "There's been no sign of your brother."

"Maybe he hasn't gone to a homeless shelter," I said. "Maybe he's OK." It was getting more difficult to believe.

"I'm glad you think so," said my father. He turned and watched the cows outside for a moment. "Herod always was different. Sensitive. You could tell he saw things in a way no one else did. Even when he was just a kid." He looked up and I could tell the barrier had slid back into place like a sheet of bulletproof glass; we were divided again. "So. I need to talk to you. Your class teacher told me about the money, Jack. And the TV."

I felt like I'd swallowed a lump of ice.

Dad stared at me, frighteningly calm. "Mr Trelawney is concerned you're funding a drug habit, but I said there was no way you'd be that much of an idiot after what happened to your brother. I'm right, aren't I?"

I nodded. I wanted to throw up.

"Luckily for you," Dad went on, "Mr Trelawney's not interested in involving the police. He just asked me to make sure it didn't happen again."

"It won't," I said, quickly.

Dad just nodded. "I know it won't." Why was he so chilled? Last time we'd met he'd whacked me across the face. I'd have almost preferred that to this sinister calm. He was planning something.

"And there's something else," he went on. "Isn't there? You left the school grounds today without permission, I hear."

Bethany.

"Listen," Dad said, "you don't hassle a girl when her family have said they don't want you hanging around. That means you leave her alone, OK?"

I stared at him. He was making it sound like I was some kind of creepy stalker. For a second, I even believed it myself. Then I remembered that half the times we'd been together, Bethany had done the planning herself.

"It's not like that," I told him.

Dad said nothing, just leaned back in his chair, watching me a moment. He reached into a drawer and pushed a sheaf of glossy brochures across the glass desk top. I stared at them, first of all only seeing the design, how similar they all were. Rosy old buildings with pointed archways, spreading green lawns, improbably attractive kids on the front wearing jackets and ties.

"I ought to have done this years ago but I respected your mother's wishes instead," Dad said. You'll have your choice of these places. I believe they all have particularly good Art departments."

They were brochures for schools. Boarding schools. "No, thanks," I said, heart pounding. This was why he was so calm. He was already dealing with the situation – with me. In his mind, the problem was solved. I would be neatly packed away, never mind the cost, and no one would have to worry about me for the next few years.

But it was as if I hadn't even spoken. "Have a look through, take your pick," Dad went on. "There isn't a whole lot of time but you'll have the chance to visit before making a final decision." He fixed his eyes on me.

I stared back. I felt cold, really shivery. He couldn't do this. "I'm not going—"

Dad completely ignored me. "You'll start in September with a hell of a lot of catching up to do, which I'm afraid is going to screw up any summer plans you had." He was going to ruin everything. I started to feel panicked, like I couldn't breathe properly. I had to see Bethany. I had to. "I understand the state system over here lags pretty far behind in terms of academic achievement—"

"I'm not going to any of those schools! You can't just turn up and start controlling my life."

Dad sat back in his chair, watching me steadily, waiting for me to finish. He was so calm. It was horrible. "Take the brochures – you'll need to put together a shortlist by the weekend."

"I'm sorry," I said again. "I don't think you heard me. I'm not changing schools."

He got up and walked around the desk so that we were facing each other again. "The decision is made, Jack."

"Save yourself the money."

"Listen," Dad said, quietly, "I'm not an idiot. I know why you don't like me. You have good reason not to. It's not like I've been around, which is a situation I regret more than I expect you to understand—"

"Oh, stop it!" I shouted. "It's too late. You're not even my dad any more. Louis is. It's not my fault you're a failure. That's the only reason you're looking for Herod and it's the only reason you're throwing your weight around now. Why don't you just fuck off and leave us all alone?"

"Control yourself." My father's voice was cold. "Do you understand me?"

"Clearly." I spoke through my teeth. "You should never have come back. Do you understand me?"

"I think you've said enough." I was being dismissed. Fine. I had the parting shot, though. "It's not just about school," I said. "You never call back, do you? There's always a reason why, but you just never do. How much effort does it take to pick up a phone?"

Dad didn't have an answer to that. There was no one else he could blame. I walked out.

Marcus and Alicia were in the hall. Marcus was holding a tray of drinks, she in the middle of talking. Her shiny, lip-glossed mouth froze. They stared at me a second. It must have been pretty obvious my meeting with the CEO hadn't been a success.

I drew in a deep breath. "Don't mind if I do." I took a cold glass from the tray and walked past them, through the sitting room and into the library. I sat down on a red leather arm-chair, staring at the glass cabinet with the ancient blue bowl, holding the iced glass to my forehead. Then I drank the lot, looking out of the window at the vines swaying lightly in the breeze. Gin and tonic. A strong one.

I was trapped in here. A prisoner.

EIGHTEEN

Sammy was meant to be meeting me in the hall outside Drama. Last lesson, Friday. Time was running out. The corridor running past the Lower Sixth Common Room was rammed with backpacks and tents. A big group of them were catching the Castle Cary train straight after school. I had a tenner in my pocket, lent by Georgie Hicks, but that was it. Nowhere near enough for a train fare: I'd have to hide in the bogs again. Not with Bethany this time. *Please, God, let her be there*, I thought. Seven and a half hours till we were due to meet, and no way of knowing if she was OK.

Sammy turned up ten minutes late, looking harassed. "Sorry, mate." He clapped me on the shoulder. "Got your wristband and ticket." Gold dust. He passed me an envelope, which I immediately zipped into the pocket of my black combats – the closest approximation to school trousers I'd found in the stuff Alicia had given me.

"Listen," he went on, "Mum got all freaked out about Bethany. You guys sharing a tent and stuff. She was going on and on about being responsible for both of you."

"Shit!" I hadn't expected to get any trouble from Yvonne. "What are we going to do? We'll have to help Bethany get in over the fence—"

"Calm down. It's all right," Sammy said. "Jesus, you're so wound up. Mum's put that mate of Bethany's down on the staff list as well. You know, the geeky one – Amelia. So Bethany's not the only girl and stuff."

Relief.

"Jack," Sammy said, "are you going to be OK for this? We're catching the train at half four."

"It's cool," I said. "I'll be there. The last two days, my dad's just sent a car, hasn't he? No Alicia. A different driver each time. When I don't turn up, the guy's going to think he's got the wrong school or something."

Sammy nodded. "Me and Jono are going home first to pick up the tents and stuff. If you don't make the train I'll see you in the Green Fields tonight." He grinned at me. "I know you'll be there, OK? Fuck them."

"OK, I'm heading out of school the back way just in case Alicia does turn up. If Trelawney or anyone asks, you haven't seen me."

Sammy nodded. "Green Fields at eleven. If you can't find

the café just ask someone. We're on the late shift tonight – you, me, Bethany and Jono – twelve till six. Mum'll go spare if she's got to arrange cover. Here." He handed me a pack of baccy, some Rizlas and a lighter. Good old Sammy.

"She won't have to," I said, and walked off down the corridor, rolling a fag as I went. I was gasping for one.

I lit up crossing the playground and walked round the corner of the Sports Hall towards the back field, savouring the delicious hit. Even prisoners in jail got to smoke – I definitely had a bad deal.

I walked straight into Mr Trelawney and my father.

A split second passed before they noticed me; they'd been talking, and I remembered they knew each other. From when Trelawney was Herod's teacher.

Dad looked out of place outside our grotty Sports Hall. You could just tell he was different: suntanned and rich, the sweet scent of money came off him in waves, despite his faded black jeans, the sun-bleached T-shirt.

For a split second I considered running for it, but couldn't stand the thought of him catching me. I wasn't about to let him win a single battle.

"Smoking on school grounds, Jack?" Trelawney sighed. "I thought you had more sense."

Dad said nothing about the cigarette, but I hadn't expected him to. He just narrowed his eyes slightly, reading me again.

* * *

"I'm sorry, Jack," Mum had said on the phone, "but this time I agree with your father. I really don't think you should go to Glastonbury. There's too much going on and to be honest you've just been so irresponsible I'm afraid something awful will happen. Maybe next year, OK?"

Even Louis was no good.

"No way, I'm not getting involved. This is between you and your mum and dad. And to be fair, it's not exactly as if we feel we can trust you at the moment, is it? This is your fault, Jack. I'm sorry, but you'll have to take the consequences."

I wasn't going to get any help from Mum and Louis.

I stared back at Dad, unblinking. Heat rose from the playground, radiating from the shabby brick wall of the Sports Hall. Had Dad guessed what I was about to do? Why come otherwise? He'd seen no reason to before now. All the same, I wasn't about to let him sniff out the acidic, burning panic slowly snaking up my throat. OK, this made things a lot more difficult. It was going to take more than an hour to reach Oxford by car. Then I'd have to get myself onto a train without him knowing.

"So, see you next week, Jack," Mr Trelawney said, and I realized he must have been speaking to me for a few moments already. "Try to sort out your uniform by then, OK?" He turned to my dad. "It sets a bad example to the younger kids, that's the problem. He'll need his books, too.

They're due to hand in a project before the end of term."

"It'll be arranged."

Well, at least now I knew Dad was a pretty cold bastard to everyone, not just me.

The car journey was silent. Neither of us said a single word. Dad didn't even put the radio on and I wasn't about to. Before the night ended, I needed to pull off some pretty audacious moves. I'm an idiot but I'm not completely brain-dead. I know when to keep my head down.

Ten minutes later, things really didn't look good. We pulled up outside the house and went in, still silent, Dad stepping back to allow me in first. So extremely courteous of him.

For once, there was no sign of Alicia, or the Labrador.

"Come into the kitchen," Dad said. "I want to talk to you."

Oh, great. I followed him in, again thinking how surreal it was that my dad's kitchen had been featured in a national newspaper. He leaned against the shiny stove. I still hadn't seen him or Alicia cook anything. The food each night just seemed to appear from nowhere. Salmon and steamed potatoes. Steak.

"I know you were meant to be going to a music festival this weekend," Dad said. *Ah. Here we go,* I thought. "You must be pretty angry at me by now, Jack, because obviously I'm not allowing you to go. But I'm not doing all this to be an asshole. I hope that one day you'll understand. People are worried about you."

I think I preferred silent and nasty.

I shrugged.

"I know what I would have done in your position," Dad went on. "And just so you know, there's no way you'll get to the train station tonight. Don't bother trying."

OK, I'd got the message. He'd be watching me.

He changed tack. "We've got some interesting people over tonight. A guy called John Hannigan from Sony. Maybe next year we'll get you tickets for a couple of the big US music festivals. Burning Man. Lollapalooza." I understood the implication: *If you toe the line now.* The thing was, he'd made a mistake treating me like his personal lapdog, ready to come whenever he called. He'd made an even bigger mistake slapping me across the face. It's the kind of thing that turns you off a person. Makes you feel uncooperative. And a year's a long time.

I was due to meet Bethany in six hours: the most important thing of all.

I had to be there.

"OK," I said. "OK." I didn't even lie. It was the hypocrisy that got me, but I didn't ask why Dad was filling his house with "interesting people" and basically throwing a party if he was so worried about Herod.

By eight, the library was filling up with old gits clutching cocktail glasses and I had begun to descend into a state of panic. The hours were slipping by but every time I moved, the Labrador, Alicia or one of my father's corpse-like friends would be right behind me. It was like I was being followed and, who knows, maybe I was – I wouldn't put anything past my dad. I lost track of how many boring questions I answered about school; I got cornered by a scary woman from the BBC who wanted to know "how you young people *really* communicate" (er, like, by talking, with our mouths?); a journalist from the *Guardian* wanted to know if I would review teenage novels for their books section. It was like being trapped in a very weird dream, all the more so because of my mounting panic that I'd never get away. I was never going to be in the Green Fields by eleven, at least, but I hoped like crazy that somehow I'd make it there before our shift finished so I could explain everything to Bethany.

And then there was a knock on the door. I think I was one of the few people that actually heard it; the buzz of voices was getting seriously loud by that point as the corpses downed their cocktails.

"Yes, so what we'd probably do is maybe send you one title a month, no pressure, but it'd be great to know your thoughts, and obviously it'll look great on your CV," the *Guardian* journalist was saying. Her breath smelt of salmon canapés and fizzy wine.

"Sounds brilliant." I grinned at her. "I'm really sorry but I think I just heard the doorbell."

I glanced around the room. Dad had his back to me, deep in conversation with Alicia and the wrinkly old dude from Sony. The Labrador was nowhere to be seen. The coast was clear. I made for the door, terrified that at any moment someone would grab my arm and I'd be "introduced" to another old crone with halitosis.

I let the library door close behind me. If I could just make the last train to Castle Cary I'd still be there in time. There had to be a way. The doorbell rang again and I broke into a run. If anyone else heard it I was screwed. This was my only chance.

I skidded to a halt on the marble tiles by the front door and heaved on the brass handle.

"Evening."

I stood and stared. Owen was standing on the doorstep with Natasha. Once again she was all red hair, shiny teeth and legs. She was wearing a billowy top this time; she looked much more pregnant. I couldn't believe Owen was going to have a kid.

"Hello, Jack," Natasha said. "Are you OK? You look a bit stressed."

They swept inside, smelling of woodsmoke and something expensive and burnt-sugary (that was Nastaha).

"Is the old man all right?" Owen asked, as if it was perfectly normal to find me here. "Whenever Herod decides to turn up, I'm going to kill him. Dad's been going round every homeless shelter in London. Christ, the amount of hassle this has caused everyone you wouldn't believe."

"Oh, no." I stepped back, letting them past. "I can believe it all right." I wondered if Owen knew about Mum and Dad being called to identify a corpse. I fought off a mental image of Herod lying cold and white in a hospital morgue, a nurse going through his pockets, trying to find a wallet, ID.

Owen raised his eyebrows at me. "I need a drink."

"We can't stay long." Natasha smiled at me again. "But O really wanted to make sure your dad was OK. He's really worried, isn't he?" It was weird: the way she spoke about my father was kind of familiar, as if she knew him pretty well.

"Really worried." I couldn't keep the sarcasm out of my voice. "So worried he's having a lovely party."

I moved towards the door. It was ten to nine according to the hall clock. The last train south was just before half nine. If I left now, I might still make it to the station.

Quick as a falling stone, Owen put out one hand, barring the way with his arm.

"Wait."

Surely *Owen* wasn't part of my Dad's scary entourage? Back-up for the Labrador and Alicia?

I had no choice but to lay out every single one of my cards. "Please," I hissed. "I haven't got time. I'm trying to get to bloody Glastonbury. He's come over all heavy and won't let me go. He's being a complete cock. The last train's in half an hour. Seriously."

Owen and Natasha looked at each other, speaking without words.

"Please," I said again. "This has nothing to do with you. I need to meet my girlfriend there. I haven't even seen Dad for nearly two years and now he's trying to control my life."

"You're going to do it anyway, aren't you?" Owen said, still leaning against the door. "You're going to try getting there one way or another?"

I glanced at the clock. It was nearly nine. I was running out of time. "What do you think I'm going to do? I'll hitch if I have to."

"Owen?" Natasha was looking uneasy.

Owen sighed. "Oh, God. When he finds out, he'll kill me. Listen, we're driving down tonight. Natasha's sister lives in Pilton – she gets free tickets."

I stared at him, not even daring to hope. They were going to Glastonbury. Of course they were.

"O?" said Natasha. "I don't want to be a spanner in the works, but isn't this just going to make things even worse for Ed? He's in an utter state already about Herod."

Owen rested his hand on her arm. "True," he said, "but you don't know Jack. If we don't take him, he'll go anyway."

Natasha shrugged. "Oh, you're all the same. OK, he's probably better with us. I just feel sorry for your dad, that's all."

I stared at them both; I hardly dared believe it.

Owen laughed at me. "Look, do you want a lift or not?"

NINETEEN

Fifty miles outside Oxford, we stopped at a garage. A safe enough distance, Owen said, but to be honest I felt like even the moon wasn't a safe enough distance from my father after what I'd done. Owen filled up with diesel, thirty quid's worth at least, and stopped inside to use the phone. I've often wondered where Owen gets his money – surely he was too proud to take it from Dad? Had he broken the pact? I've never asked. He was inside for a few minutes, then Natasha and I watched him run back across the forecourt with a bulging carrier bag. I could hardly breathe. What if Dad threatened to call the police? What if he tried to follow us? I wouldn't put anything past him.

He wasn't going to take this lying down.

I shut my eyes, dreading the moment Owen got back into the van.

Natasha turned to me. "She must be a pretty amazing girl. I hope this is worth it." She wasn't just trying to be a bitch, either. She meant it.

"So do I." I glanced at the clock on the dashboard. Quarter past ten. Bethany would still be expecting me to meet her at the Veggie Café. What would she do if I wasn't there?

What if Dad had talked Owen into turning around and driving back again?

Owen swung himself up into the driver's seat and tipped the contents of the bag into Natasha's lap. Prawn cocktail crisps, cans of Coke, a Ginsters pasty. M & Ms. Road food, basically. We were going.

"Don't get me wrong," Owen said. "He's furious. But it's cool, don't worry."

I took one of the Coke cans and drank it in gulps, cold sweetness pouring down my throat. "What did he say?" I managed to croak, once I'd recovered the power of speech.

Owen was already pulling away across the forecourt. They're so alike, Dad and Owen. Both totally ruthless. "Nothing." He flipped on the indicator, hauled the Sprinter out onto the slip road. "According to that poodle-boy assistant of his, he was too busy to talk to me. He said to call back tomorrow. Must have guessed what happened, that I took you with me."

We were being frozen out.

Owen laughed. "Oh, well, looks like that's me out of the will, then."

I held the Coke can to my forehead, leaning back against the seat, staring at the snaking line of lights before us, the road slipping away and away every second.

We'd won and Dad knew it. He wasn't going to destroy his dignity by chasing after us through the night.

I wondered if I would ever see him again. A man with three sons, and all were gone.

Eleven came and went; the night slipped past the windscreen and I wondered what Bethany was thinking. Was she annoyed? Hurt? Waiting for me? Her dad was dying: I should have been there for her.

We left the van and Natasha at her sister's house, a huge converted barn in a pear orchard just outside Pilton. The sister, Louisa, was like an older, posher version of Natasha, only her hair was more washed out – peachy rather than bright red – and she wore a nasty fake velvet headband and a girls' rugby shirt with a turned-up collar.

"You must be Jack!" She smiled at me. "Wow, you all look so alike. So much like Ed."

What? Natasha's sister knew my dad?

I glanced at Owen but he just shrugged. "Jack's a bit fazed," he said. "Had a long day. Thanks for having us, Lou."

"Don't be silly, it's lovely you came. Real shame you missed the headliners, though." Louisa didn't appear to have noticed the shockwave that passed through the kitchen when she mentioned Dad's name. She smiled, offering round glasses of red wine. "Who was it, anyway? I'm glad the tickets are being put to good use this year. Rob and I just can't be bothered with it! Owen, are you really going down there tonight? Aren't you just absolutely shattered? Natty, you look dreadful. You should have a bath and go to bed."

"Thanks," Natasha said, winking at me.

Owen gave Louisa the full-wattage smile. He's always been like that with women, he's like a bloody hypnotist. "All the more reason to stretch my legs. Coming, Jack?"

He kissed Natasha; we left the warm, wine-filled house and went out into the lanes, Owen and I. He rolled a joint and we smoked it; I wondered how many times Owen and Herod had been out on the prowl like this, side by side, when I was just a kid, not part of it. Now I was there and Herod was gone, but it was like I could feel him there with us, another person, only just behind, just out of sight, hidden.

"You're quiet," Owen said. I could see the fence through some trees now, battered corrugated iron. The night was filled with music, light. One hundred thousand people and more. The biggest party on earth.

"Yeah." I couldn't stop thinking about what Louisa had said: *So much like Ed.*

"Not all of their friends took Mum's side," Owen said. He shares Dad's creepy ability to see what you're thinking sometimes. "Tash and Louisa's old man was friends with Dad from their first day at uni. He and Mary never liked the way

Mum made it so difficult for Dad to see us once he'd left."

"Did she?"

Owen shrugged. "It was a nightmare. Don't you remember? When we went down to London, it was because she'd kept thinking of reasons why we couldn't see him. OK, so Dad was the one shagging around – it was his fault they broke up – but even though he was meant to be able to see us whenever he was back in the UK, Mum always had some excuse. He nearly took her to court, but everyone said it would be pointless because of his job. We wouldn't have been living with him anyway, just away at school." He blew out a cloud of smoke, shrugging. "It was a mess, really. I don't know if I blame Mum or not. Lou is Dad's god-daughter – that's how I met Tash. She was travelling after uni and stayed with him a couple of weeks in San Francisco. In that amazing house with the pool – do you remember it?"

"What?" I demanded. "So while you were away, you saw Dad the whole time?" I couldn't get my head around it. Over the past five years, Dad, Owen – and Herod, too – had retreated out of my life, sticking around in my brain like faded photographs of themselves. In the meantime, Owen and Dad had been seeing each other. Just getting on with it. I suppose the truth is I was jealous.

Owen shrugged. "Not the whole time. But once we went to Burning Man and afterwards he said there was a girl he wanted me to meet, an English girl who was staying with him—"

"What?" I said. "You went to Burning Man with *Dad*?"

"Yep. He's good friends with the guy who started it back in the eighties."

I stared, trying not to imagine my father off his face at a crazed festival in the Nevada desert. Gross.

"Anyway," Owen said, "so afterwards I went back to San Francisco with Dad. I hadn't seen Tash in thirteen years." He smiled. I understood about that.

What more was there to say?

"Come on," I told him. "Let's go." But when I turned to look at him, it was as if he didn't see me but someone else, a long time ago.

"It's my fault," he said. "I know all this is my fault. Herod couldn't take it. I knew but I didn't want to know. I was having too much of a good time. Simple as that. It was my fault: I didn't look out for him. I should have opened my eyes. I was the only one who could have stopped him, and I didn't." He sighed. "I don't even know if it would have made any difference – whether he would have got ill, anyway – but at least I would've tried. Not just let it happen, like a complete idiot. He was meant to go to art school – he's a total genius, and instead, he's been hanging around in that creepy retreat for the last few years. Wasted."

And then I said what I'd been thinking since the moment I knew Herod had left the Peace Centre. "What if he never comes back? What if he's dead?"

Owen stopped, leaning on the corrugated-iron fence

with one hand. "I first came here with him in 1990. We saw Pop Will Eat Itself and I threw up about nine pints of cider. Couldn't drink it for years after that. We lost each other about five times but we always used to meet up at the Stone Circle and mess ourselves up on hash brownies. It feels like such a long time ago."

Owen sighed. "Herod's not dead. He's still here. I just don't know where." He shook his head. "Come on, man. Let's go."

I followed him.

TWENTY

"Family Camping." Owen nodded at the nearest signpost. "Where are you heading?"

"Green Fields." I looked around at the sea of tents, the glowing lights. I could just see what must have been the Pyramid Stage through a bank of trees, and a helter-skelter. Silk flags fluttered. It was a temporary city, a crazy place. Wild excitement shot through my veins.

"Other side of the site," Owen told me. "I'll come with you. There'll be a load of people up at the Stone Circle. There's still the same lot coming here." He laughed. "You go away for five years and nothing changes. It's where we always meet. Green Fields is on the way."

And so we walked through the city of cities, past camp-fires, middle-aged women dancing by a hedge with no clothes on, hordes of people completely out of their minds, grinning, laughing. The main acts had finished but there was music everywhere still, the night was bursting with it. The smell of weed and sewage. Lights pulsing through night-black tree branches. Silk flags flapping hard in the wind. Dried mud beneath our feet. Strings of coloured bulbs lit up stalls selling pancakes, chips, garlic mushrooms, noodles, dodgy tie-died clothes, smoking kit, camping gear for the unprepared. It was uphill to the Green Fields and I followed Owen; I'd have been lost without him. He seemed to know where to go without looking at any of the hand-painted signposts. It was twelve-thirty when we reached the Veggie Café – a bigger set-up than before. Old rugs laid out on the floor, people sitting at low wooden tables outside the main tent. Moroccan lamps flickering everywhere. There was a queue.

"I'm late," I said to Owen. "They're going to kill me."

He laughed. "See you later. I'll come back for a free tea – make sure you're all right."

"You don't need to look out for me," I said, but he was already loping away into the night, off to find his mates. I watched him go, a tall, ragged figure, moving quick and quiet like a cat. Here one minute, gone the next. Always the same.

Sammy was behind the counter, taking cash and looking harassed, shouting tea and coffee orders over his shoulder to Jono, who was wearing an oversized jester's hat complete with bells. Idiot.

I pushed my way to the front and just kind of stood there

till Sammy looked up and saw me. He stared for a moment.

"Fucking hell." He passed a Styrofoam cup across the counter, spilling hot tea over his wrist without seeming to notice. "You did it. You actually did it."

And then he cheered, and so did Jono, who took off his deeply embarrassing hat and threw it in the air. They cheered and surged out from behind the counter and bearhugged me. They must have already been quite wrecked but I didn't care. I'd made it. I was here. I'd done it. And then everyone in the queue joined in the cheering, too, and a complete stranger passed me a joint. That's Glastonbury for you.

Bethany wasn't there.

"She turned up just before eleven with that Amelia girl," Sammy said, handing me a slab of carrot cake to slice. "Must have left about half an hour ago."

I stood there holding the cake. "You told her to come back, though, didn't you?"

Sammy shrugged. "Yeah." He frowned. "She was meant to be working, wasn't she?" He glanced at his watch. "Obviously not, though. Mum says this happens every year. We always end up short-staffed. It's bloody charming – we even managed to get her mate in on our staff list right at the last minute, no ticket and everything. Now they've both buggered off."

I knew, I just knew, that something was wrong. Bethany wouldn't do that to Yvonne without a good reason.

The joy and the sheer thrill of it all drained out of me,

the adrenalin, the energy. I stood slicing cake mechanically, staring at the white wall of the tent. A kitchen in a marquee. After that it was washing and chopping lettuce, tipping it into plastic crates, pouring water from a heavy jerrycan, adding a handful of salt. Jono, the jammy git, had got the best job, flipping Yvonne's home-made veggie burgers on the barbecue outside, the air was rich with the smell of charring food, icing sugar, cigarette smoke, coffee.

I didn't see Bethany till three in the morning.

I was mixing icing for the carrot cake when I felt a hand on my shoulder. I turned around and she was standing there wearing jeans, her black wellies and a big purple cardigan fastened with a butterfly made of beads. Her hair was in two plaits over her shoulders but the fringe was hanging in her eyes. The plaits were fastened at the ends with beads and feathers. She smiled but even then I knew. She didn't move towards me. I knew not to touch her. She was separate, apart from me already.

I glanced across the kitchen, saw geeky Amelia standing on the other side of the counter. Waiting for Bethany. They weren't planning to stay.

A rush of sickness shot through my body and I had to draw in a long breath, staring down at my hands, one gripping the spoon, one holding the bowl of icing sugar and cream cheese. Both hands dusted with icing sugar, sticky with lemon juice.

I was the first to speak. I suppose I thought it would be

easier on Bethany if I did. I didn't want her to suffer. Instead, I brushed off my sugary hands on my jeans, suddenly feeling claustrophobic.

"It's not going to happen," I said, "is it?" And I wanted to shout, *Why, why, why?* And, God, I know everyone says this but it's true: it hurts, it actually hurts – a physical pain in your chest. When the moment was over I knew it would only get worse, because the next day I would wake up and she'd be gone, it'd still be true. The day after that, too. For ever. The weight of it pressed down on me; I felt like I couldn't breathe. I couldn't stand it. "Why?" I asked. "Just tell me why." I half knew already. There was only one reason.

Bethany shook her head. She was crying now, crying a lot, but silently, leaving trails of black eye make-up down her face.

"Dad's not going to get any more treatment. There isn't any point. We found out yesterday. He told me to come here, though. He insisted." She laughed, face covered in tears. "He virtually forced me, got Mum to drive me and Amelia to the station. Said it was my time to be young. I don't even feel like it. But Dad's not the reason I can't see you any more, not really. It's Mum. She was so upset about that stupid party and now… For once, I don't want to wind her up." Bethany smiled, sadly. "She's a mess. I told her and Dad I wasn't going to see you again so I could concentrate on school next year. I just want to make them happy. I just—" She stopped talking, tears streaming down her face.

"Please don't," I said. "Please don't cry."

"The stupid thing is, I wanted to come here so much and now all I want to do is go home. I just want to ring Mum and get her to pick me up. But Amelia was so excited. I can't leave her here on her own."

"Bethany—"

She shook her head. "Jack, when I said I loved you, I wasn't lying. I was telling the truth."

But it didn't matter. She was still finishing it. Her dad was going to die and she was finishing it with me to please her mother. The pain intensified. It felt as if my insides had been gripped by a giant hand, squeezing tighter and tighter.

"I know my mum can be a bitch," she said, quietly. "but this is hard enough for her as it is. I'm sorry. I'm really sorry."

"No," I said. I couldn't help myself. "Jesus Christ, Bethany, there's got to be a way." My dad was probably never going to speak to me again and I'd done it all for her. I was desperate for her to stay.

Bethany shook her head. "Don't think I haven't tried to figure it out, Jack. I've tried to think of a way. I just can't do it at the moment. I've got to think about them. My parents. You don't understand: I'd do anything to make this easier for them. My dad's going to die. Really soon." Tears were streaming down her face. "I'm sorry." She shook her head. "I know only I'm fifteen and everyone says we're really young but you know what? I'm never going to feel like this about someone again. I just know."

I wanted to beg. I honestly could have. *Don't make her*

feel guilty, I told myself. *Don't go down to her a bitch of a mother's level*. I couldn't forget the look on Bethany's face when her mum caught us at the party. *You're making all of this worse, Bethany*. Blaming her. Bethany had looked like she'd been kicked. She'd been made to feel guilty enough, manipulated into doing her duty, the right thing – as that woman saw it. I couldn't do the same; I was sick with rage. All I could do was back off and make it as easy for Bethany as I could. Score the moral victory. It didn't feel good.

"It's OK," I said. It wasn't. "I understand." I felt it in the pit of my stomach, like I was going to throw up. I had to tell her. "You'd do anything for anyone no matter what, and that's why I love you, all right? You're amazing."

Bethany smiled, sadly. "I'm not amazing," she whispered.

"You are, you are."

We held each other for the last time and, God, that was one of the worst experiences of my life; that total mad joy, the feeling of being really myself, complete, knowing that I had to let go of it and watch her walk away. So I pulled back first, letting go of her hands last of all.

"I'll still see you around," Bethany said. She rubbed her eyes, streaking her face with black eye make-up, silver glitter. "Won't I?"

I shook my head, gathering hold of myself. I don't know how I managed to get the words out, keep control; I felt like screaming. "I don't think we should."

Even then I wanted to hold her so much that I had to

ram my hands into my pockets. Seeing her across a room, at someone else's party, was going to be far worse. Better not to. Better to burn fast, like this, get it over with.

"Oh. Oh." And Bethany didn't say anything else, just turned and walked away, through the kitchen. Amelia was waiting, put an arm around her shoulder. They passed Sammy and Jono still serving customers at the counter, who turned to stare. Then they walked off through the tent, out into the night.

Bethany was gone. Lost in a crowd of a hundred thousand people. Gone for ever.

"Jack?" said Sammy.

"Leave him alone," Jono muttered. "Poor bastard. Women." Even then he was acting so worldly-wise I wanted to punch him.

I didn't, though. I just walked away. Out of the kitchen, through an open tent-flap, through the cluster of staff tents and away.

I never knew where the next three hours went. I walked alone through the crowd for some of it – past the Dance Tent and into this weird American diner place where they were hiring out ballroom-dancing outfits. I was never going to see her again. I knew it had to be like that. OK, it was a small town but we had different friends. It wouldn't be hard to figure out which parties to avoid.

She was gone, and here was I at the biggest festival on

earth, alone. Had it really been worth the sacrifice? I would probably never see Dad again. I'd be written off. He'd forget about me, and all for nothing. It was light when I found myself up in the Green Fields again, legs aching. I'd been walking for hours. I couldn't face Sammy and Jono yet, so instead, I headed up to the Stone Circle, weaving my way through clusters of people sitting around and smoking weed, drinking, laughing, shouting. I leaned against one of the big standing stones, staring blindly out at the festival below. It was just a mass of colour, of light.

"Hey, want a lift up?"

I turned to face a skinny guy with a dyed green beard, beanie hat pulled down low over his eyes. "You look like a chap in need of perspective," he said, with the uncanny insight of someone who has taken a lot of substances in one night.

I shrugged. "All right."

The guy gave me a shin up and I sat on the stone. Before I could thank him, he was gone. I stared out over a valley full of light, strands of smoke moonlit-silver. I rolled a fag, but smoking it didn't change anything. I felt as if I'd broken open like a dropped egg.

She was gone. Bethany was gone. At last, one of us had done the right thing. The sensible, mature thing. But it didn't feel right.

I closed my eyes, wondering what was going to happen when all this was over. I had to face Dad at some point.

You've been an idiot. I'd come haring down here with Owen and all the time Mum and Dad didn't know where Herod was, if he was even still alive. Now I'd stuck the knife in again, twisted it. There were payphones here somewhere, had to be. If I called first thing then at least Mum wouldn't worry about me any more.

What was Dad going to do when I got back? Would he just disappear to Tokyo or San Francisco or Paris or New York, and I'd be forgotten again? His bright, shiny boarding-school brochures seemed kind of appealing now: the idea of going somewhere new, far away from her, from Bethany. *You must be desperate, then,* I thought. What a loser. I remembered what Jono was like when he broke up with Dani Smith just before Easter. *She's minging, anyway.* He said it to anyone who'd listen. But I could never say that about Bethany. I couldn't hate her, and it only made everything worse because I still wanted her, didn't I? Just couldn't have her.

"Jack, is that you?"

I couldn't help jumping. I turned. Stared.

At first, I thought the person looking up at me was Owen. It wasn't. He had longer hair and he had an earring too, like Owen, like Dad, but his was a small green jade hoop. He was wearing a ragged sweater, jeans and brown workboots.

"Herod," I said. And then I had to say it again. "*Herod.* What are you doing here?" The sight of him knocked the breath right out of me. I literally couldn't believe what I was seeing, so I just sat there, utterly helpless with shock.

Herod smiled, as though finding me sitting on a massive stone pillar at Glastonbury was the most ordinary thing in the world. They're all the same: Herod, Dad, Owen, moving along in a different stream to everyone else. "Jack," he said. "Kismet: fate. I had a feeling I might see Owen – we always used to meet here – but it's you. Wow. You look so much older since Christmas."

I stared at him, cigarette burning down between my fingertips. I looked into his eyes. Was he really there?

Herod looked back, just him. The Creature was gone. For now, perhaps. But it was gone, all the same. This was just Herod. He'd beaten it.

Herod smiled at me and I laughed; I couldn't help myself despite the weight of misery in my belly. He reached out with one hand and I took it, sliding down from the stone. "What are you doing here? Man, you should call Mum."

"Why? I was going to call on Tuesday, after all this." He stared at me, frowning. "What's wrong? Is she OK?"

I couldn't believe what I was hearing. "You've really got no idea," I said. "Have you? Listen, two weeks ago, that girl from the Peace Centre rang to say you'd gone missing. Mum and Louis were in France. She called *Sabine* in Paris. They came home early."

"Shit," Herod said, very quietly, shutting his eyes a minute. "Andy. I should have guessed. I'm such an idiot. I really didn't think she'd do something like that. I thought she had more sense."

"They think you're ill again. Mum's completely freaking out," I said. "Dad came back and everything. He was in Japan and he flew over a week ago to look for you." I told him about identifying the body, the homeless shelters, the calls to every hospital they could think of. "What happened?"

"Oh, my God." Herod sighed, pushed back his hair. "It turned out Andy wanted us to get together. I've never thought of her in that way. Didn't reckon I'd led her on or anything. It was pretty awkward, but I'd been thinking about leaving the Centre for a while, maybe going to live in France." He smiled. "It's easier to live on the dole and be an artist over there. Anyway, I left sooner than I was going to, before I'd really spoken to the others about stuff. Dave and Simon were away on a retreat when it all kicked off, so I just told Andy. I really didn't think she'd do something that stupid." He sighed again. "Bloody hell. I'm here doing meditation workshops for Simon's cousin. He's got a yurt. He normally comes down here but his girlfriend's just had a baby and they didn't want to waste the pitch fee. I said I'd come and do the classes for them."

Herod had left because of Andrea. There was nothing wrong with him. "But Mum and Dad must have called the Centre a hundred times in the last two weeks. It's been searched by the police, for Christ's sake. Why the hell didn't Simon tell them you were taking his cousin's bloody yurt to Glastonbury?" I demanded.

"I told you – Si's on a retreat. In Thailand. He doesn't

even know I'm here. His cousin lives in the Peak District – I had to go up there first to pick up the yurt. He hasn't been down to the Centre in months. Nobody there knows where I am." Herod groaned, shaking his head. "Dad came back. Are you serious?"

Then Herod looked up, right at me. "Jack, are you all right?"

In my mind, I saw Bethany walking away from me through the café, past the crowds waiting for coffee and chai. She was gone. She was gone.

"It's just this girl," I said.

Herod watched me for a moment, saying nothing. At last, he spoke. "Maybe one day she'll come back."

But I couldn't think like that. Slow torture. Always wondering.

She was never coming back.

"What are you going to do?" I asked, and Herod said, "I'm going to find a phone."

And then he asked me, "Are you coming?"

So I went with him, walking side by side through a city of tents, the odd café still trading, selling flapjacks and tea; a guy in silver trousers offered us hash truffles from a tray hanging around his neck, but instead we bought beers from a woman pushing a cool box in a wheelbarrow. They were still cold. Herod paid for mine and we walked on, drinking cold beer in the early morning light, just me and Herod.

TWELVE YEARS LATER

I stop the van in the traders' field and check my phone. The reception as usual is crap down here but Sam's texted saying he'll meet me on site. He's been down since Monday; it's Wednesday now and finally the book cover from hell is off to the printer. Done. I'm free and it's just as well. This is our last chance to get the van anywhere near the café and it's loaded with sacks of dried chickpeas, industrial quantities of apple juice and some shifty cash-and-carry cider for the staff; if Sam runs out of anything else we'll be wheelbarrowing it from the traders' car park, like it or not. The site manager's not as strict as Glastonbury but it's not worth the hassle.

Christ, it's hot. The place is like a dust bowl already, a rash of tents spread out across the sweeping front lawn of a stately home. I drive slowly with the hazards on. A guy staggers across the roadway wearing what appear to be brown leather hot pants and nothing else except a weird feathery thing around his ankle. It's eight in the morning; I was first in the cash and carry after leaving London at six. At least there was no traffic but it's not as if I'm going to get any more sleep for the next three days. It's not that kind of festival, even if you're working.

"Nice one, Jack." Sam staggers from his tent just behind the kitchen; he must have heard the van. It's knackered. You can hear the bearings squealing in the next county but the old girl's got a few miles left in her yet. Owen sold the Sprinter to me for a hundred quid after Tasha and Aoife put their foot down last September. "Dad," Aoife said. "You've got to stop driving that thing. It's just embarrassing. Get a proper car." Her mother agreed. Owen got the better of both of them by selling the Sprinter as ordered, and buying an old red Post Office van off one of Herod's mates instead. Em creeps out of the tent after Sam, rubbing her eyes.

"Argh," Em says, taking Sam's hand. "You should have been here last night. It's not even meant to have started yet." She smiles, pushing back her hair. "Insanity. Pure insanity." They're good together, Em and Sam. Yvonne's freaking out over the wedding, even though it's not till the end of September. I'm meant to be reading something in the church; I just hope it's nothing too slushy. Sam getting married. I can't believe it. It seems so ridiculous, somehow.

"Come on, let's get some tea on," Sam says. "We can leave the stuff in the van, use it as an extra dry store."

Anyway, the café's pretty quiet. Just a few people sitting around drinking chai and smoking. Its always like that, this time of the morning at a dance music festival. No one's going to want a full-on breakfast till the early afternoon at least.

"I'll get us a brew." Sam slopes off behind the counter to the kitchen, starts messing around with the urn. A brew. He stayed in Manchester after uni and he's talking like a northerner now, or maybe that's just because he's around Em so much.

"So, was it an OK drive?" Em says, then frowns slightly. "Do you know that girl? She's staring at you."

"What girl?"

Em looks away in a failed attempt at subtlety. "Dark hair, that table over near the blackboard." She grins. "She's definitely got her eye on you, Jack."

I turn, look at the blackboard first: a chalked-up list of prices. Tea and coffee £1. Chai £1.50. Veggie breakfast £6. Home-made cakes £3. I can't read the rest because there's a girl sitting with a group of mates in front of the board. Em's right. She's looking right at me.

She looks different, but not different. Her hair is shorter, for one thing, hanging loose around her shoulders, pinned back behind one ear with a silk flower. And she's wearing a totally ridiculous white dress that looks like something off a Greek statue, with wellies.

Years. It's been years. The last time I saw her was at that party just before everyone left for uni, and she was going out with an arty guy from the sixth-form college with bad hair and pretentious jeans.

She's here now, though. We look at each other. My mouth's gone totally dry. Suddenly, I don't feel tired any more. I get up, head spinning. Not enough sleep and too much driving.

"Beth?" says one of her mates. "Are you OK?"

Without even thinking about it, I'm checking out her friends. A mix of girls and blokes. Do any of them lay claim to her? *Don't be so ridiculous*, I think. *Don't be such an idiot*. But anyway, I'm walking towards her, and she's standing up now, too, in her dusty white dress with a silk flower behind one ear.

"Hello, Jack," Bethany says, smiling.

And not for the first time I think how funny it is the way when I see someone from school we hug and kiss each other on the cheek, and how unimaginable that would have been back then. I mean, you just didn't. So we do it anyway, the polite hug and kiss on the cheek. But instead of the usual pulling away, the usual questions – *So, how are you doing? Have you seen so and so*, and all that crap – we don't let go. We hold on to each other, and the whole tent is staring, but I don't care because she's here.

Bethany, at last.

ACKNOWLEDGEMENTS

Thanks to Denise Johnstone-Burt, Ellen Holgate, Nic Knight and the rest of the Walker team, and also to Catherine Clarke and Will Llewellyn. I'm very grateful to Annette Boxall, a Wyld Mare always, for giving me some helpful advice about police procedure, Jamie Cornwallis for explaining how to make a rose and Rosie Wellesley for the medical tips.

Thanks also to Steph Hinde for getting me that job in family camping and to Jules Jenkins and Bubsie Yates for employing me as their fry-up chef.

BIOGRAPHY

Katy Moran lives in Shropshire with her husband and two sons. She has written three historical adventure novels, but this is the first book she has set within her own lifetime. She has worked the graveyard shift at many festivals, and can dig a trench through a flooded kitchen whilst icing a cake, reconnect a broken electricity supply, make six cups of tea and fend off customers who want to climb across the bar and help – all at half past four in the morning.